THE WIFE

IRIS IMENEO

Tellwell Talent
www.tellwell.ca

ISBN
978-1-77302-833-0 (Hardcover)
978-1-77302-832-3 (Paperback)
978-1-77302-834-7 (eBook)

FOREWORD & AUTHOR'S THOUGHTS

Society has lost much of its sense of the family unit along with a strong belief system, faith as it were.

Additionally, technology and the media have supported the creation of monsters.

Technology serves to provide instant gratification to its users (Segue here, since we're all users does that make the big tech companies the pushers? After all, the cyber-world is ultimately addictive.).

We live in a world where people never need to leave their abodes.

Groceries, food, liquor, medicine, healthcare, clothing, personal items, absolutely everything a person might need can be delivered right to your door from the click of a button. You can get an education, even a university degree, via online distance courses. You can play games and see the world through cyberspace. There are even jobs that don't require you to leave home at all. Contracts and documents can be sent and signed electronically. Banking, payroll and bills, can all be processed online. This causes a social disability because people are no longer required to navigate being out in the general public. Think about that for a moment. What kind of a person would you be if you never had to cross your threshold to get out into the world at large?

Next, let's talk about specific social interactions. You can meet anyone on social media, become their "friend", text, Skype, etc. without ever meeting them. Couples have gotten married without ever having set eyes on one another. They met through cyber-space, communicated electronically, shared pictures and stories which may or may not have been altered or embellished – after all, who would know? As these "relationships" progressed, perhaps they spoke verbally. After they liked what they'd learned online, found the other person's voice pleasing and seemed copacetic on the beliefs front, and perhaps even engaged in intimate tech-sex, they decide to get married while meeting in person for the very first time. Now, think about that for a moment. What kind of a marriage is delivered out of that dance? You just married someone and have no idea if they're a slob, or if they have hygiene issues, or the opposite. Do they take up the whole bed? Do they do their dishes right away or leave a mess in the sink for someone else to clean up? What if they turn out mot to be pleasing as a mate in person? The only thing missing here is the chance to get married online without ever meeting in person. Maybe it's already there and I'm too disconnected to have heard about it. Is it a long stretch to think that you could meet, date, get married all online without actually meeting, and then decide to have children by adopting some poor youngster or orphan also online? Predicatively, what does that mean for the next generation? How screwed up will they be as a result? I challenge you to reflect on that for another moment.

So now we've established that there are really fucked up people out there who live in complete social isolation, very different from the way our generation and our parents grew up. After all, we still leave the house and derive joy from meeting new people, selecting our own produce, perusing racks of clothes and shoes, going to the park, having meals out, etc. Now, let's layer on even more complexity by factoring in the media.

Don't get me wrong, we need the media to bring us news of what's going on in the world, what the weather is going to be like, and a plethora of other information. The format has changed, going from radio to newspapers to television to the web. Television is still the most common medium for the older generation, the newsfeed for the younger of us. We're like Pavlov's dog in the sense that we automatically know which channel or url has weather information at our fingertips, which channels and urls have news running all day and all night long. We used to read news updates weeks after the events happened, that shifted to days, then the next day, to now instantly. Wars are fought in real-time.

Tragedies are brought into our lives minutes after they happen. So the format has changed, the delivery time has changed, but also the content has changed. When I was growing up there were words and images that never made it into our homes. That naiveté is lost now. In general, our society is desensitized more and more over time. The more provocative and disturbing and gory the story and its images, the better. Then, after being instantly captured into the story, with our social deviants in some form of ecstasy for a little while, we move on to the next one.

Now I want you to take a moment to think about the person who is socially incapable and who has a constant feed of (for them) very titillating human events in the world, all in real-time. Is it any wonder there are a growing number of sociopaths in our society, some of whom end up in the ever-growing pool of psychopaths? True monsters.

If you've been wondering about where my diatribe is headed and what it has to do with this book, here you go. In this book, you're going to get a glimpse of the impact such a monster has on regular, normal people like you and I. We should be taking on the challenge to drive change in our world to stop creating more deviants, to find ways to stop the rapid production of more and more of these types of people. Otherwise our "normal" will become a minority.

I'll step away from my pulpit now and let you know that this is the first book in a series I will be writing. I've had a delightful time writing it because it's been a lifelong dream for me. My editing of the book is (for me) the most tiring part as I like to just get things done, and editing is all about going over the same stuff again and again to make sure you got it right. I am appreciative of my husband through this process. He's been excited about the book. He's told people I'm writing it. He's been a source for content when my imagination has failed me. He's been an inspiration for me to understand the true meaning of family, marriage, and parenting since those pillars of knowledge and meaning were largely non-existent in my own life. He asked me one night to read him what I'd written so far. It was my first rough draft and I only had about ten chapters done. When I got to the end of the tenth chapter I looked at him and said, "That's all I've written so far honey." He looked at me (I can't even begin to describe the look) and he said, "Well you can't just leave me hanging like that. I want to know how it ends!" I told him I wouldn't tell him. And then a few weeks later offered to read him the next set of chapters. His consistent reply to that question was that he would wait and read the book once it was all done. I've had fun writing it. I know my husband liked the beginning, so I'm pretty sure he'll like the whole book. He deserves acknowledgement for his love, support, and ideas on this project. I love you for that my handsome husband!

Now, dear reader, get comfortable and enjoy. Take a little walk with me.

Be careful of the monsters you meet. Understand your risk when you invite them in. If you read this book and then wander to look in the mirror, with wonder, and truly really reflect, "Am I a monster too?" If you answered yes, then think about that. Long and hard.

Regardless, it's time to take a little walk with me.

This book is dedicated to my husband.

Thank you, Vito.

Know that I love you wholeheartedly.

BELIEVE

In a world that is fast becoming soul-less
Be challenged to find your own soul
Then make it self-less.

When the television portrays only tragedy
Be challenged to turn it off
Spend your time working on your own humility.

If you're surrounded by people who are envious
Be challenged to cull the herd around you
Fill your life with those who bring joyousness.

During the times you feel utterly hopeless
Be challenged to claw your way out
Understand that genuine happiness is timeless.

Find your soul.
Believe in yourself.
Trust in your God.
Love your family.
Share your plenty.
Lean when you need.
Live out loud.
Love heartily.
Grow your humanity.

Infect the world with your faith.

ONE

CURRENT NIGHT

The insects were thick and noisy and busy around his face as he sat there in the dense jungle foliage. They were so very loud too. It was pretty much all he could hear. And they were biting him like crazy. He had never imagined being in a jungle in his life, let alone in the dark and this far out from any semblance of civilization. He couldn't slap at any of the bugs for fear of making a noise. "Bloodthirsty fucking insects" is what Gabriel was thinking in his own head. He thought about every book he had ever read and how they described the jungle as having a life of its own. He had scoffed at those descriptions from the comfort of his own living room. From where he came from there was no way trees and bugs and other creepy crawly shit constituted a life of any kind. He squirmed around in his spot, quietly, as much as he thought he could under the current circumstances. None of his ruminations deterred the night creatures in any way shape or form. He hoped the persistent attackers would spear themselves on his five o'clock shadow that was well past the five o'clock mark. At least that brought a slight form of a smile to his tired face. His legs felt like they were on fire underneath him but he dared not move. He was hot in his clothes, far too hot, but he couldn't remove them either. Imagination brought thoughts of being cooler, but also being attacked more ferociously without any protective clothing on at all. Gabriel sighed heavily. His sweat continued to soak the inside of his clothes. He heaved an even heavier sigh as he weighed his emotional reason for being here.

Nothing else mattered. Time to suck it up. Wait. Today was another day. Would it bring any answers? He hoped and prayed, maybe a little bit more today than any other day.

Regardless of what he thought or imagined, he couldn't move in any significant way. He couldn't swat at a single one of those mother-fucking bugs. He had to be almost perfectly still and quiet. He had to focus on his mission. And his own personal goal. No matter what this dark night brought to him, he had to keep his focus. The jungle creatures continued to make constant and infuriating noises around him. He felt things crawling on his skin and was afraid to even think about what species they were. He really hoped there were no other beasts in this jungle hell hole he needed to contend with tonight that weighed more than a few ounces to a few pounds. Even though he wore a long-sleeved army regulation shirt and army surplus pants, these mother-fucking insects were biting through his clothes to get to him. He worried about the other predators that could bite through fabric and what issues they'd cause him. "Stupid jungle", thought Gabriel to himself. "Why am I here?" He asked his questions silently and in his mind, but it was only because he could make no noise. Besides, his questions were rhetorical. But for crying out loud, why couldn't this operation, and the others he had been on, go down in a clean bug and rodent free shopping mall in Minneapolis or LA or somewhere decent? He would even prefer somewhere in the Arctic where the most serious predator was a flipping penguin protecting his egg between his legs waiting for Mommy to come home from her swimming journey with all of the other mommies? Or a rabid wolf in the middle of Nebraska that didn't know his head from his tail and thought Gabriel looked like a decent meal. Room service in fact. He could handle being bitten and having some of his parts gnawed off, okay, and maybe he'd even bite back a little. Beyond the biting monster insects, Gabriel felt something move across his military boot as he was crouching down low in the foliage. The cicadas were deafeningly loud. The monster mosquitoes were biting hard and furious. And now this thing crawling across his foot was probably a fucking snake. And Gabriel hated snakes with a passion. Always had. His whole life. His mother used to hack them into tiny little pieces when they came into her garden. Hack them up with whatever was around. A shovel. An ice-breaker. A pair of scissors. A knife. Whatever was there. She was always so concerned about her precious garden. Then she'd make Gabriel scoop up the little dead pieces and put them on the compost pile where they would stink and rot. His mother would say it was a message for the other serpents not to trespass into her garden. Well, after many years, the message wasn't working so well for dear old mommy and her fucking garden. She was dead and buried in her fucking garden. She had always said she wanted no fancy funeral where people showed up that mocked her while she was alive and then pretended to like her and miss her after she was dead. She just wanted to be buried in the dirt with no fancy coffin and hoped that over time the worms would turn her into compost. Well, she got her wish after the cancer and other ailments finally killed her (Lord have mercy, but it took a long time of watching her complain and making the people around her suffer). She was buried about six feet under in her garden with no coffin and a simple cotton sheath. With her beloved worms. And, as Gabriel well knew, to this day, the snakes continued to have free reign over her grave, slithering to and fro as they pleased. If snakes could smile, Gabriel was certain that they were busting a gut laughing and she was probably rolling over in her grave, mind you not her coffin since she didn't actually have one, since she couldn't hack those serpents to death anymore. Gabriel sighed heavily. Mommy was dead, and not by snake bite. But dead she was, and he missed her. It wasn't the end he would have wished for her, but then again what proper son would have wanted that kind of an end for his mother, really? She did manage to look after him all of his life, especially with the asshole of a father he had had. She was really tough at times, but then also so gentle when she sensed he was a lost soul and needed a special kind of mother's comfort. He never ever doubted that he was her little boy and that she loved him more than anyone else on the planet including herself. She would rather give up her food or her life or anything in between to make sure he was whole – mentally, emotionally, and physically. Whatever it took. Gabriel still loved his mommy and always would. Time to refocus now. His mother was in a place where he could no longer help her. He needed to help the other key woman in his life. Refocus. Now. Okay. Time. He checked his watch again. Then, just waited.

Gabriel wasn't certain what kind of snake was slithering over his foot right now. Probably poisonous. Especially in this hell hole. What else would be here? Gabriel continued to hold still until the stupid thing was off of him. He figured that was a good technique as opposed to startling the thing and having it bite into him. Then he'd have to die in this God forsaken place with no conclusion...other than being dead. The thing had to have been at least three feet long given how much time it took to cross completely over his boot. Gabriel secretly wished he could have hacked it into tiny little pieces the way Mommy used to. But that wasn't an option. He had to be perfectly still and silent until his ear bud microphones gave him the all-clear to go ahead with the rescue. The jungle was alive around him, as it would be with the other guys on the team. The sounds, the heat, the biting critters, and other enemies they hadn't even thought of yet. He wondered how they were all doing. He knew he would be last to go in today because this operation was about him and not them. Gabriel wondered if this time there would be answers for him. Three years. Other operations. Tens of thousands of dollars. Other hell holes. Time. Money. Training. Three years. No answers. Would he find any answers today in this jungle armpit outside of San Paulo? Would he finally know what the hell happened to Lillian? They had told him three years ago that she was gone. Dead. But when he went to the scene to find his proof, there was none. The scene was horrific. It was the content nightmares and horror movies were made of. They had tried to hold him back to spare him. But he went anyways. The carnage was brutal and disturbing. It was followed by a visit to the morgue a few hours later after they finished asking him nine million questions for which he had no answer. Gabriel would never forget that night for as long as he lived. It was a memory that would never fade.

He reached into his pocket as quietly as a mouse and touched the only fragment and remnant he had of her. From that night. That terrible night. His world broke apart right there and then. He caressed that small patch of red cloth in his pocket from the gorgeous red dress she was wearing that night. The one she had worn especially for him. He had so many questions. So much time had already passed. With so few answers. Although his heart was broken, shattered, he tried to keep the man together because the man needed closure. He needed to know. He longed to hold her in his arms just one last time if that's all there was to be.

Gabriel was broken out of his reverie as voices buzzed in his ear. Louder than those fucking insects in this hell hole. It was time to move in closer. He needed to focus. He needed to stop wallowing, at least for a little while so he didn't put his cohorts in any jeopardy. Time to go. Time to move. Focus. He held back as he thought of her. Would he find Lillian tonight? Would it finally be over? His darling angel? Or at least would he garner enough answers so he could put this ordeal to an end once and for all? Time to focus. Time to listen. Voices buzzing. Time to go. Move. Listen. Rescue. Extract. And kill along the way if need be, if anyone was in his way.

Was it going to end tonight? Would it be her? What would the answer be? As he rose and started to move he thought to himself, "I'm prepared. I'm ready. I'm strong. It's time."

Gabriel moved quietly through the jungle, at least as quietly as he could. His hair was damp with sweat. His clothes were even more wet and stuck to his body. He stank from the sweat, but more so from the adrenaline coursing through him and out of him. He was on high alert. He took no joy in his surroundings. If things had been different, perhaps he and Lillian could have come to a tropical place. Warm. Sultry. Beautiful. With awesome flowers and vegetation and smells. They could have walked hand in hand along a soft white sand beach. Enjoyed sunrise and sunset and midnight walks. Good food, good wine, compelling conversations and, last but not least, great sex. And Lord knew they loved each other, and they loved each other's company, and they loved to laugh and explore and experience together. They were two grown adults with all the benefits of being adults, but at the same time they were like a pair of little kids just having fun together and playing together. Oh, his Lillian was a delight to him. Such a special creature, pretty in a non-traditional way. Quirky in her own weird way. Sexy. Smart. Edgy. Those three words really summed her up. What he loved most about her beyond all of those things though was the fact that she was an empath. She understood things by feeling, whether it was herself, or a situation, or the person/people around her. She felt, truly and deeply felt, for people. He respected that about her, but it also caused problems. Because she felt so much and carried such tremendous emotional baggage with her, she was misunderstood. People didn't get that she was like a child in some ways. Smarter than the average bear – for sure. But naive in some ways of the world. She sincerely wanted to help the people around her, especially the ones closest to her, and somehow that caused her to trust people unconditionally. She took them at face value and they took information from her that often condemned her. An emotional child in a grown woman's body. The most wholesome intentions with the worst delivery on the planet. If the road to hell was paved with the best of intentions, Gabriel didn't doubt he was on the expressway of that road with his beautiful Lillian. He sighed again, heavily, just thinking about her now.

The jungle vines pulled hard at him as he moved forward. The sweat continued to trickle down his spine. Probably at this point it was all running down into his boots because every stitch of clothing he had on was already soaked. He thought to himself, "Fuck the insects...they are never going to give up until they have a blood transfusion big enough to support the entire fucking planet of their species."

He needed some answers so he could put this ordeal to rest, once and for all. It was time to focus. It was time to move. Gabriel needed to listen. He thought to himself, "I hate these fucking snakes and bugs. Fucking jungle hell hole."

He moved as silently as possible through the jungle foliage. The same as the rest of his team mates. Ears alert to the sounds coming through his headset as well as the jungle itself. It wouldn't do to be eaten by a jaguar. Not only would he have no answers, his teammates would probably talk about that for all eternity. Embarrassing. Even if he was dead at the end of it. An extra-large mosquito swarmed around his open ear. He wanted to swat and squish and kill the motherfucker but knew he had to maintain control and silence. The lush vegetation gurgled and sucked at his boots as he walked toward his next goal point. Gabriel kept his eyes alert for any other motion in the jungle. He had a good sense of where the other two guys were, but needed to stay tuned in just in case there were unfriendly participants in tonight's mission.

He thought to himself, "Lillian, my love, where are you? Why did this happen? Why did it have to happen? Who did this? Why am I here? What in the world is going on? Honey, I just wish I could will you home." With that, Gabriel touched the cross on the chain around his neck, looked up at the heavens, and prayed, "Dear God. You know what she means to me. How can you put me through this ordeal? What have I done so wrong to deserve this? What has she? Whatever it is, please give her back to me in one piece and alive. I will fix everything else in my life that's wrong, but please let this nightmare end and please let me have her back or at least allow me to have some closure that I know she's sitting in Your living room now and waiting for me to join her. Please God. Please. Please. Please." Gabriel sobbed silently because he had to maintain radio silence. The tears streamed down his face. He was tired and weary from this entire endeavor. He desperately wanted to go home. With his wife. His little contrived family. And hide from the world. All of them together. "God. Please. Help. Me."

A few moments later Gabriel's ear buds vibrated with a voice and some instructions.

It was time. Time to go. Time to move. Keep focussed. Go get some answers.

Gabriel made his way further forward.

TWO
SEVEN YEARS EARLIER

Mrs. Johnstock walked into Gabriel's office and announced with some reproach that Ms. (not Miss or Mrs.) Lillian Capwell was here to see him. As Gabriel sat back in his ancient brown leather chair, he took a moment to inventory Mrs. Johnstock. She had been his secretary for quite a few years now and still he didn't even know her first name. She was in her late fifties. Glasses always on a chain around her neck. He wasn't even sure if she ever put her spectacles on or if they were just there for decoration or intimidation. She seemed to be a big-bosomed woman but that was probably largely due to all of the "just-in-case" tissues she kept in inventory there. Gabriel thought she was a pretty stern old bird. Always wore a proper dress, hemline below the knee (in fact Gabriel might even wonder if she had any knees), collar was up to choking standards, and there was no way any of the fabric could inspire a man to do anything more than make a tablecloth and serviettes out of it. Mrs. Johnstock always wore her clip-on earrings. A different pair for each day of the week, although the same ones for each day of each week in perpetuity. Regardless of her somehow staunch manner, she was highly efficient. She never gave him attitude, other than her old biddy kind. She kept him organized and shuttled people around like nobody`s business. And he almost always got out of there on time at the end of the day because of her. She shut people down and sent them off to wait for another day. Yes, she was a gold mine. For an assistant.

It did however make him wonder about Mr. Johnstock. Gabriel knew nothing about the man. Had never even met him. Enjoyed many a moment to himself wondering if the surname had any reference to the man himself. Of course he wouldn't dare to approach Mrs. Johnstock with any of his reflections or musings. Gabriel returned his focus to the present moment. Sat back up a little straighter in his chair. Cleared his throat. Steady gaze full forward.

"Thank you Mrs. Johnstock. Please show her in, in about five minutes. I have a few things to clear from my desk first, and then I will be ready to meet with her. You know, confidentiality and all that these days. By the way, do you have any idea what this is about? Did she say anything at all when she made the appointment?"

Mrs. Johnstock's starkness took hold as she declared there was nothing she could tell Gabriel about his next appointment. The woman had made the appointment, advised it was a private matter, refused to provide any details upfront, and had clearly gotten Mrs. Johnstock's "goat" as it were. He could tell by Mrs. Johnstock's demeanor that the woman waiting to meet him was at least pretty, if not sexy. Mrs. Johnstock did not like women who were not buttoned up to the neck and covered well below the knee, assuming they had knees. Anyone not fitting those criteria she did not like at all. She cleared her own throat, albeit more satisfactorily than Gabriel had moments before, and then advised him, "Certainly I will give you five minutes." She then turned around in an almost military fashion and walked away from his desk. Stiff backbone. Straight as a fucking rod. Almost as if she had one strapped permanently to her flipping back. Gabriel watched that back walk confidently as it strode out of his office. He smiled and sighed heavily at the same time. Then he focused on organizing and clearing the papers strewn across his desk. He mused to himself while he worked, "Who was Lillian Capwell? Not Mrs. Not Miss. But Ms. And what was Ms. Lillian Capwell here to see him about today? What did she want from him?" Gabriel knew pretty much everyone on town after all of these years, but her name was unknown to him. And, on one hand, he could name any person in this remote place who might possibly (and possibly is a huge stretch) want to call a meeting with him and meet in his stuffy office sitting on the uncomfortable chairs for as long as it took to get their issues out.

"Well," he thought to himself, "there is an old adage to consider. Curiosity killed the cat, BUUUUUUT, satisfaction brought him back!" He figured at least his sense of humor would guide him through.

"I guess my five minutes is up" thought Gabriel as his office door opened. Gabriel looked up and was floored. He saw the bluest eyes ever. And a very pretty woman. Not model swimsuit rock star drop dead gorgeous. But very well put together. Clearly fit. Looked like she worked out. Flat stomach. Possible abs. Fairly thin, but somehow strong looking. And she was tidy. Purposeful for certain. With an element of something he could not put his finger on. Yet. Something. Dark ...No. Dangerous... no, maybe. Elusive...possibly. Cautious....one hundred percent for sure! Special and unique...guaranteed.

The air in the office seemed to drain out with Gabriel's thoughts. This was a first. For sure. But, as a testament to the man his mommy raised, Gabriel bucked up and manned up. Then he stood up, with his old office chair creaking along the way, and he reached out to shake her hand. Her handshake was cool and somehow dignified, and very firm. If Gabriel had at that moment had any line of sight to the course his life was about to take he probably would have told her to get the fuck out of his office. But premonition was not in his DNA.

Gabriel sat back down again into that old office chair. Creaks abound.

The moment he looked up again into those blue eyes, with a shadow of grey, Gabriel was mesmerized. He thought to himself, "Who is this woman? Why is she here to meet with me? What does she want? Why? Why? What?"

Then Gabriel choked out with some difficulty, trying to camouflage his lack of confidence, "I'm Gabriel. It's a delight to meet you. Won't you please sit down and let me know how I can be of service?"

A very pregnant pause followed. Lillian's steel blue eyes laid into him. She assessed him from the other side of his scarred desk table top. She was clearly making a decision. Then she made her decision, he thought. Because she sat down. Formally. Uncomfortably to some extent. This was clearly not a woman used to asking for anything from anyone. She swallowed hard and gave Gabriel one of the toughest looks he had ever seen in his life. The she said, "I need your help."

From that moment on, he was lost.

THREE

JUST OVER THREE YEARS AGO

Life was pretty good. Not great, but how is that even possible when a few people get together? Gabriel and Lillian had made quite a number of adjustments in their lives. And some compromises. And some really fucking hard decisions along the way. Gabriel had grown to understand the choices Lillian had made in her past. And the history as to why she'd made the ones she had. There were things that he found out about her without her disclosure which caused him to understand her saga and suffering even more. He had been diligent in keeping her past hidden and discreet from anyone else in this community. Vigilantly. Silently. Quietly. Even Lillian didn't know to what lengths he was sheltering her. But she deserved it. Finally in her life, he hoped he had delivered peace to her. He reached out to people he really didn't want to know in order to make sure her past stayed far away from her. Gabriel did so behind her back. He wanted to keep all of the past ugliness and chaos as far away from Lillian as possible. It almost became a mantra for him. And he felt she deserved it.

Whenever he had a quiet moment he wondered, "What is it about her that makes me want to help her? Connect with her? Better yet, Stay with her?" Gabriel was so far out of his element but he knew he loved this woman. And that he wanted to spend the rest of his life with her. At this point, today, the wolves were at bay. Was he enough of a superman to her to protect her long-term? Gabriel had no clue as to what had hit him almost four years ago. And Lord knew he was way out of his realm then. Not to mention now. Gabriel had recruited people he didn't even want to know to keep those wolves at bay and make sure Lillian was protected. Lillian had no idea about the work he had done to in order to do so. Gabriel had been covert about all of it. He felt there was no need to trouble her even more than she already had been in her life. Gabriel intended to keep everything away from Lillian. Only on that front though. With every other aspect of their lives he gave her one hundred percent transparency.

As he awaited her return home from work, he contemplated and reflected. They had made a very lovely home together. A family, albeit a strange one, but a family nonetheless. They had all moved in together into this lovely southern plantation home, complete with the "Tara – Gone with the Wind" massive white pillars. Every time Gabriel walked out to their wrap-around veranda, he was stunned by the grounds. They rented out some of their fields to sugar cane and cotton farmers. At least that helped to pay the taxes on this huge old place. Close to the house were these beautiful Magnolia and weeping willow trees. They brought shade and flowers. Beautiful swaying branches when the wind blew through. White and pink flower petals when the hail hit in late spring and broke the blossoms off of the trees. Beyond that, a small orchard. They were in the south after all, so peach trees and cherry trees were a given. But they also had a modest group of apple and pear trees. And two rows of Mulberry trees which Gabriel had always wanted, running around the outside of the orchard like a border. All of these trees bore fruit every year which he and Lillian found ways to preserve. Jams and sauces. Frozen. Vacuum packed. Sealed and sterilized. They did it all. On the agenda for next year were fig trees and lemon trees. Orange trees never really interested either of them. And you may as well play baseball with grapefruits too as far as they were concerned. There was a fair sized garden on the western side. Tomatoes, potatoes, onions, nine varieties of hot peppers (well maybe not that many, and for sure they were not all hot), beans, peas, corn, lettuce, and items that Gabriel had never even experienced in his whole life. But that was no big surprise...all his adult life he had shopped at the supermarket, not gone out to the yard with bowls and scissors to collect items for the evening meal. Then, as you came around the corner a little further, there was the small fruit patch. Grape vines on a beautiful trellis. A raspberry and blackberry and blueberry patch that kept encroaching further and further on the yard. The strawberry patch just a little further beyond. The yield from these fruit plants was astounding to Gabriel. Especially as he and Lillian worked side by side to diligently preserve their bounty in freezers and mason jars in their cold room.

And then there were Lillian's flower patches. Of course Lillies, and some Irises, bleeding hearts, and peonies. Lillian had an affection for beautiful flowers. She couldn't grow roses to save her life, but the flowers she did grow blossomed under her care. Gabriel loved watching her tend her flowers. It was one of the few times that he saw her totally at peace, completely relaxed. Her hair would be tucked up underneath her sunhat. Gardening gloves he cajoled her into wearing so her hands wouldn't get rough. She'd prune and cut and trim and transplant, sometimes for hours on end. He'd be tired just watching her, yet he'd bring her a cool drink and revel in her accomplishments watching the satisfaction on her face as she stepped back to look at the progress with him. He had to admit that she really did bring their landscape to life.

Mostly, the alligators and serpents Gabriel severely disliked stayed further down by the swamp in between the cane and cotton fields. Gabriel always shuddered as he got close to that section. He wanted no contact with any of those vile creatures. Lillian was a little hardier than he was on this front, but he knew she didn't like them so much either. But she did take control when those beasts got into her precious chicken coop or some of the other livestock they were growing. Gabriel chuckled as he figured that by now any crocs or snakes knew they'd be turned in a purse or boots if they fucked with Lillian in any way shape or form. The chickens were diligent in producing the eggs they ate every morning for breakfast. Gabriel and Lillian took the older chickens over to a local (gentle) abattoir when their time was up. They left them respectfully in their freezer for a while before consumption. Their roosters crowed every morning, unless it was too cold, and they had little chicks to keep the cycle going every spring. The rest of their livestock was made up of a few cows for milk and butter, horses for fun when they went riding, a couple of pigs for bacon and ribs and such, plus a few other varieties for their own personalities.

When the gardens and livestock didn't need any tending, Gabriel and Lillian spent their time inside their old mansion. First, they were like little kids running around and discovering the treasures hidden in closets, the attics, under sheet covers, etc. all around the place. Each new-found treasure brought them a sense of joy and glee. They spent many an afternoon with a couple of glasses of wine as they cleaned and polished the items they'd found and spun stories of the circumstances or functions where those items were used, how they came to be in their home, what their history was. Gabriel and Lillian also plastered and painted and renovated. To many people it would have been an endless chore. Go room by room and reinvent it. By your own hand. With count-less trips to the local hardware paint and lumber store (just one store fits all in this neighbourhood unless you wanted to drive about three hours to find a big box store). But they loved doing the work. They loved working together. Work. Progress. Music as they worked. A kinship and alignment of heart and soul that was very new to the two of them. But it worked. Just fine.

Then there was the decorating. Not your Sears catalogue stuff either. No way. No how. They had spent so many weekends and holidays and escape moments over the last years hunting for their special things. Unique treasures for each and every room. In fact, as they developed the rooms, each one ended up with its own theme. Whenever Gabriel looked around and wandered through the finished rooms, he could pretty much identify where each piece came from and when they had acquired it. Many pieces had their own history and he and Lillian often took the time with the previous owner to learn about the piece. Some stories were sad. Some stories were heartbreaking. And some stories were happy, but those were few and far between. But all of these new pieces were now making a new history in this old historic mansion, which also had a history of its own. Somehow, a little disturbing, and not far removed from Lillian's own history. Strange, maybe. Spooky, for sure. But Gabriel had both feet planted firmly on terra firma and didn't subscribe to all of the southern mumbo jumbo. He was a religious man, for sure, however he didn't give any credence to the voodoo and evil spirit stuff that was resident in this area.

It was almost six p.m. now. Gabriel wondered where Lillian was. She really should have been home by now. Hopefully she would be in another few minutes and then they could get started on their dinner as a family. Gabriel sighed as he walked restlessly to the front windows, again. It wasn't like Lillian to be late and not to call.

A very unsettled feeling came over him while he gazed out of the front window waiting for her car to drive up. That feeling didn't dissipate as he wandered back to the kitchen to monitor the food. His foreboding thought was, "Something's not right."

FOUR

CURRENT NIGHT

Gabriel had three other men working with him on this mission, two in the field with him and their team leader on lookout. As they approached the house, there was one man on each side of him. Their leader was monitoring and directing everything. Gabriel by now knew each one of them personally. And they knew his trouble and strife. There were no secrets in this clan of misfits and broken down men looking for answers. Each one had his own story. Sad. Angry. Betrayed. Whatever. Maybe just plain old hurt. They were a team, by now, of mercenaries. Of sorts. Not the usual kind of religious zealot mercenaries or the kind of guys who went out for hire for big bucks to assassinate some dude. A set of guys who worked to resolve close, personal problems where the law couldn't and wouldn't go. A place where Gabriel never imagined he'd be. Not in a million years. Yet here he was, with a set of very unlikely compadres of a sort. Nothing he ever expected. Oh well.

The jungle hummed and buzzed around all of them. The snakes slithered on the ground and hung from the trees just waiting for an opportunity to bite or kill something. The insects were all equally ferocious. Some deadly and some not. But Gabriel tried not to think of them. Just tried to tune into the other sounds around him. And hear what their leader was telling them. And what the rest of the team was doing, where they were. Gabriel thought about the other two guys on the jungle floor with him.

There was Joe. A rough guy. Ready to rumble and tumble at a moment's notice. Rough around the edges. Constant five o'clock shadow. Scars on his body none of them ever wanted to ask him about. Eyes were brown and so very dark they might as well be black. Muscles abound. The hardness within him was palpable. And, from what Gabriel knew, understandably so. What a history that man had. And still he overcame it. Gabriel wasn't certain he could ever stomach or deal with what Joe had gone through. And beyond that, to come out and do what he did now on a regular basis? It boggled Gabriel's mind. It really did. Joe was on Gabriel's left. Swarthy, steady, quiet, and ready to proceed further as soon as he was told. Gabriel knew for a fact that Joe was not afraid of anything on this planet. Monster. Man. Mouse. Or anything in between. Joe would just deal with whatever came his way. If he died or his obstacle died, that was just "life". That man really did roll with the punches.

Frank was on Gabriel's right. Mid-thirties. Blonde. Blue eyes that could just drown a person. They were soft and sensitive, yet hard and unforgiving at the same time. Out of the two men, Gabriel related more to Frank than Joe, likely because he was the more approachable of the two men and a bit more of a chatty-Kathy. Regardless, they'd been together for quite a few of these operations, and that kind of experience created a very tight bond. The men's lives depended on it.

As instructed, the three men approached the mansion. Gabriel breathed heavily in anticipation as he moved toward his side. Crickets and other Godforsaken insects buzzed around his head and exposed body parts. The insects seemed so very loud to him, but that was understandable in the current situation. Gabriel and the others were all on high alert. Their adrenaline was pumping. Gabriel wondered if this mission would result in any answers for him. And then, if he did have answers, would he be able to live with them? Some tough questions, but not the first time he'd asked himself those questions. And the same applied to the rest of the crew. Gabriel knew some of their answers, but his own story desperately needed an answer.

The insects and other vermin continued to buzz and slither around Gabriel as he used his large knife to cut through the jungle greenery. Even though he wasn't aiming for anything Gabriel hoped he killed more than a few of those slithering snakes as he slashed through the trees and brush. Hopefully he was taking out a few giant insects along the way. He edged closer to the mansion, seeing that the lights were mostly on. The lawn looked manicured, so obviously in this hell hole the owner had some money. As per the plan, Gabriel crouched low in the damp grass or weeds or whatever the heck they were and stayed as still as he could.

As he and the others waited for their next instructions to be barked out into their headsets, Gabriel reflected on what had happened with Lillian a few years ago. It felt like a lifetime ago. What had gone wrong? Where was his Lillian? Why did this happen? He had been so careful with all of his questions and investigations. She should have been safe. Was this random and thus had nothing to do with her past? Gabriel had no idea what to think. But perhaps tonight would bring him some answers. He hoped. As he waited. And his thoughts alternated between moving forward tonight and that night a few years ago. Where was his beautiful Lillian? He loved her and missed her terribly. Although other people scoffed at him, he brazenly and proudly told everyone she was the love of his live and his soul-mate.

"Lillian, I love you so much, and I miss you so much. Please help me find you. God, please help us if you can." Gabriel pleaded and prayed.

FIVE

THAT NIGHT JUST OVER THREE YEARS AGO

Gabriel wondered as he wandered through their old mansion. "Where is Lillian?" He prowled their home restlessly. She should have been home about two hours ago. It just wasn't like her not to call. Or answer her phone when he called her. He stared out of their front window yet again. The stained glass window they had installed together on the side wall window enhanced and amplified the setting sun. That had been such an amazing day. Finding the stained glass. Measuring it. Understanding that it fit perfectly for where they wanted to place it. Bringing it home so carefully, almost as though it was a newborn baby. Carrying it in. Figuring out how to install it properly. They even had to Google for additional instructions beyond what the guy they bought it from told them to do.

But then Gabriel came back to tonight and wondered, "Where was she?" as he kept looking out and longing to see her headlights come down the road and up the driveway. As he waited and worried, he reflected on her history. He knew there was a great deal of anguish there, some of which clearly kept her awake many nights. He'd wake up and she would be out of their bed. She would wander through the old house at all hours of the night. Get a glass of water. Sometimes something stronger to take the old memories and put them further at bay so maybe she could sleep for a little while. Gabriel could never understand the old memories she had nor how they continued to keep haunting her. Lillian had nothing to fear from him, yet she still feared. A lot. Often. He had never laid a hand on her especially since he knew she had been abused beyond what she'd told him. And she never would talk about those things, he knew. She was both proud and ashamed. And she knew that people tended to take another person's vulnerabilities and find a time and place to hold those against them. Gabriel prayed that he never hurt his Lillian by reflecting back to her the heartaches and the decisions she had made in her life. He knew his words could wound her to her very core. He'd seen the look under other circumstances. Saw her tears well in her eyes. Saw her straighten up. Pull back. Lock down. Another piece of her he would never really know or comfort or delete from her history. She was a woman who protected herself in silence and a shroud of self-abandonment. People mistook her stance as a lack of self-confidence or self-flagellation when what it really was, was a position of self preservation.

Gabriel gave his head a shake and thought about the rest of Lillian's nocturnal wanderings. Her footsteps through their old house. She would look at their accumulated treasures. The beautiful things. He thought about her sweet smile. Like a little girl when she found a special treasure. The endearing look to him to visually ask if she could have it. Would he buy it for her? Lillian had a special propensity for flowers. But not the ones from the florist. And most certainly not the ones from her garden. Porcelain or feathers or Murano or glass flowers. Something that would not die. Lillian had had too many things in her life that died. Live flowers were for the gardens. Flowers for the house had to be endless and beautiful forever.

On her nocturnal wanderings he knew she would think about their times spent together. She often shared her thoughts when she came back to bed. Sometimes wake him up just to talk. Many times she'd think he was sleeping and just talk to herself. Gabriel would pretend to sleep just to hear her open-hearted little girl musings. Some nights she would be quiet. The silence would bother Gabriel but he knew enough to leave her in peace. He knew she was thinking about her past and the decisions that had led her there. In those times she would get out of bed more often. She would simply use one of the many restrooms then grab a glass of water and then wander as quietly as possible back to their bedroom, slip off her bathrobe, and crawl into bed. She was his wildflower and he needed to let her sleep in peace. Often he would watch her while she lay sleeping. The old words from an old song always came back to him, "Let her cry for she's a lady, let her dream for she's a child." Many nights Gabriel stayed awake to try to make sense of her sleep-talking. He had pieced together a few of her past horrors along the way and they chilled him.

Gabriel knew Lillian had not had an easy road through life. Somehow he hoped that his relationship with her and his love for her would lessen her burden. Yet so often he looked into those stunning blue eyes and he saw a kaleidoscope of emotion. Love, for sure. Compassion, no doubt. Empathy, without question. Gabriel knew his Lillian was an empath. A real live one. It freaked people out because she was also somehow psychic. He reflected that people wanted to know what they didn't know. Other people wanted to know what they really shouldn't know. Others still wanted to know what they already knew but really didn't want to know. Lillian's sensitivity and messages often made her an outcast when she shared her talents in an unbridled and innocent fashion, like the untethered child she really was within. Her gift, however, brought her an emotional link to people that both charged and discharged her. Her talent drew them in. Their needs drew her in. Ultimately it exhausted her. Everyone else left surprised, baffled, happy, or sad.

Gabriel knew that Lillian would give you her last dollar if she thought you needed it more than she did. Cliché – yes. But so very true. How many times had he witnessed that? But beyond the mushy feel good stuff there was an impenetrable steely resolve to this woman that would not be broken down or torn down. He'd seen that side and respected it a great deal.

Gabriel was glad she was his. He loved her. Probably beyond any sort of love she could even imagine. He loved her strength. He wanted to protect her from her weaknesses. And there were many of those. Sometimes Gabriel even wondered if there were too many for him to protect her from. The clichés kept coming back, but they were all true. She made him whole. In some fucked up crazy way. They were soul mates. Lillian was his lost rib. He sighed with longing and worry. His gaze wandered back to the special window.

Where was she? And why was she so late? He picked up his cell phone to call her. Again. Then it connected. Gabriel was stunned for a second since she hadn't answered her phone the other times he'd called frantically.

Then a man answered, "Hello."

What? What? Who? What? WTF? Did he misdial somehow? No. Not possible. His Lillian was on speed-dial. Programmed in to his phone.

"Hello." Again. The same man's voice.

Who was this guy? Why was he answering Lillian's phone?

As beads of sweat formed on his forehead and a cold chill ran down his back, Gabriel grew some balls and responded. "Who the fuck are you? And where is Lillian? And what the fuck are you doing with her phone?"

Fear coursed through Gabriel as he heard the sinister chuckle on the other end of the phone. And then there was the bone-chilling reply. One that he would not forget for as long as he lived. The man whose voice he did not know answered him back. "Sure, Lillian is here. For now. And she's not alone. I want you to think about that. For a long time. A very long time." The man on the phone sighed in a sick and happy way before saying even more. "Don't call this number again. Ever. And don't call the fucking cops either. You don't want to know the consequences if you don't obey me. Have a nice evening mother-fucker loser. Enjoy your lovely supper. I'm sure it's tasty. I'll leave you to figure out how I know about that. I have your Lillian and even more than that. Why don't you think about all of that and dream about it tonight too? Sweet dreams, buddy boy." Another sinister laugh ensued.

Then the click followed by the hum on the line as the guy hung up. Gabriel put his head in his hands. Cried out. Screamed. His shoulders shook. What was going on? Why was this man answering Lillian's phone?

Who was he? Where was she? Where were they? Did her ex grab her? It didn't sound like him from the legal transcripts she had let him listen to years ago. However if it was him, then how had he managed to find her?

Where was she?

Who was he?

What should he do now?

What?

What?

What?

Why was this happening to them?

How could that man know about tonight's supper?

Gabriel was completely baffled. Adrenaline coursed through his body as he paced frantically, trying to collect his thoughts and figure out what to do next. The grandfather clock in the hallway ticked the seconds away, echoing loudly in the big old house, that now felt more like a cage than a home.

SIX

CURRENT NIGHT

After he had cleared through the last of the jungle foliage, Gabriel stared at the mansion in front of him. It was beautiful. More beautiful than the recon pictures they had reviewed earlier in the day. It would have been gorgeous, not now, but in another time and place. There was a charm and elegance to the old stone and architecture. The craftsmanship was magnificent. Many men with talent had worked on this place. Put their hearts and souls into it. Some maybe even had given up their lives in the process as this was not a country known for safety regulations nor looking after their blue-collar workers. He gave his head a shake and wondered....."Would Lillian be here? This time?" The intel seemed good. But Gabriel had been let down before. Why would today be any different? Or would it? His musings continued.

Then Gabriel squared his shoulders. He had faith. And would live by it. Every day. Until the day he had to refute it. The there would be Hell to pay. Father, help me. Gabriel didn't ask for more than that. Either God was on his side with Lillian or he wasn't. Gabriel prayed that He was.

The insects were buzzing like crazy. Still. Non-stop.

Gabriel was instructed to cover the side entrance. By now he knew that it was protocol in these operations that the most invested person got assigned to the least critical entryway. Most to lose meant least critical access point. From past experiences Gabriel knew the reasons why for this approach. He'd seen firsthand the other opps where his compadres, the ones most invested, went in and saw the end result. Too late. Too little. Now what? The shock factor. Men broke down when they saw the brutality inflicted on their loved ones. Wives. Children. Raped. Destroyed. Tortured. Broken. From what Gabriel saw he often wondered if the ones that were left dead were perhaps better off for everyone than the ones that were barely alive. The dead could be buried and grieved for. The ones that were still alive were so damaged. Their humanity had been ripped from them. There was a vacancy in their eyes that was unnerving. There was a sense that nothing more could be done to these people than had already been done. Anything more would solicit nothing of value for the punisher or torturer. Often, dead was better than damaged for the loved ones they left behind.

Gabriel knew the current crew very well. They were a little more experienced than he was. On some of their operations other men were added, but most left when their gigs were up, when they had closure, answers of any sort. Sometimes it was a serious and heartbreaking closure. When wives and children died. Some mutilated. Dismembered. Clearly abused beyond what any of these men could ever do to a human being in their lifetimes. Especially the innocent ones. It turned your stomach. Gabriel had seen many men just break down and lose it when they found their loved ones. The anguish on their faces was palpable. Some threw up. Some vanished into a mental vacancy that would never be overturned. Some got angry. Somehow their rage fueled a different way of life when they got back to where they were from. Some just gave up and killed themselves because they couldn't handle what had happened. None of these men had a home anymore after that experience. Gabriel recalled strong men who had fallen down and broken as they then crawled over to the beaten down bodies of their loved ones. He could never forget the gut-wrenching sobs that came from deep, deep down inside these men. Gabriel knew that if they could, these very tough men would just crawl inside of the poor dead tortured bodies. As if somehow they could carry the burden of torture or simply just die alongside them.

There was a dichotomy in the responses. Some men gave up and wanted to die. Other men prayed to God. Pled to God. Cried and begged for an outcome other than what they were seeing and living.

Then there was the last kind of men. They were the ones that got very angry. The ones that went for some serious revenge. The men that came out of opps that were not recovery opps. The more dangerous kind. Those men were derailed for the rest of their lives. They ended up going to the places where they lived originally, but they were shells of the men they were before. They lacked an element of humanity. They became vigilantes. Not that the world today couldn't use some of those people for sure. Bring on the NRA! Some ended up in jail. Others were killed in gunfights or knife fights. Or in some other unforgiving scenario.

End of the day, the repeated sadness was overwhelming.

The successful missions were few and far between. But somehow when one of those came along it fed something inside this core team, it filled an appetite for hope and faith. When the loved ones were reunited, everyone cried, especially if injuries were minimal. Even the team cried. There was relief that it was a good mission and that it was over. There were happy tears because they saw the unbridled joy of those rescued. There were also tears born from their own sadness since either their own missions had not had a happy ending or their stories did not yet have an ending. It was the occasional positive result that powered the men through their next missions.

"How would this one end?" Gabriel thought to himself. He had been on a few of all of those different types of missions. Most were dangerous. Every one of them was unheartening for sure. They were worse than anything he had ever imagined being involved in during his life. All he had prayed for was a decent life. A good career. A nice wife to come home to and hold in his arms every night. Someone to kiss hello to and goodbye to and goodnight to. A soul mate. Friend. Companion. Then, when the time was right for both of them, a family. Or just a family in general if he was too old to start a new one. Love. Comfort. Companionship. Cooking. Family. Movie night. Dinners out. Holding hands. Slow sweet love when the mood struck. Peace and normality. Was that too much to ask for? Really? Why did it have to be so hard? Why did he have to be out in the middle of a fucking jungle in the middle of nowhere looking for his Lillian? Why couldn't he be home with her right now in front of the TV watching one of the silly comedies they both loved? Her head on his shoulder. Him holding her hand. Or just touching her leg. How many times had she fallen asleep on his shoulder while they did that? It made him sad that he had often complained about how heavy her head was and that it killed his shoulder while she slept on it. He'd give anything to have that back again right now. Sore shoulder or not. Why was that kind of peaceful too much to ask for? It was all so bittersweet because he'd had it all in the palm of his hand, many times taking it for granted, many times when he should have been more loving and understanding. He regretted every time he'd been angry with her and wounded her with his words or his distance. Gabriel would take everything back right now and apologize on his knees if only he could go back to that time with his beautiful woman.

Gabriel longed for the normal family life. Not this fucking around looking for his beautiful Lillian, a jungle this time, other similarly depressing places the other times. He wanted resolution and closure. Gabriel missed his wife. His little family. Dear Lord, will I find her today? Would his beloved beautiful Lillian and his little family be alive and okay today? Tears welled in his eyes. It had been so long since he'd seen them and touched them.

Gabriel's ruminations were interrupted when Liam's voice came over the headset. "Front and rear men move in. NOW. Fast and Quiet. NOW. Keep your mic's on. And for fuck's sakes, don't shoot each other when you get to the middle of the house. Gabriel, you need to sit tight. I know you want to go in. But you know the drill. You've done enough of these missions with us. You know how they go down. Trust your team. Trust me. Trust all of us. If Lillian is here then we will do our best. You know that. So...sit tight. Your job is to watch the side door in case we have anyone trying to exit unexpectedly. The rest of you guys, I want you all to have your weapons locked and loaded and ready to fire if needed. Just, for fuck's sakes, don't shoot each other!" There was a chuckle from the men, albeit a nervous one given the tenseness of the situation, but a chuckle none-the-less since that last directive was a common mantra for Liam. He repeated it very often. It was even more comical since no one had ever shot each other on one of their operations. Maybe he just said it so often knowing it would elicit a laugh and thus bring the stress level a smidgeon lower.

Gabriel started to sweat as he moved into position closer to the house. He always wanted to be the first one in on these missions but he knew today why he couldn't be. Fuck. Fuck. Fuck. It was so hard to be so close. And to be leashed like this. Would today be it? He wanted to Rambo the mansion and find his lovely Lillian. Rescue her. Hold her in his arms. Never let her go. Protect her from anything and everything. Forever. And ever.

Gabriel watched the side door restlessly. It was all he was allowed to do. He watched. The more he looked at the door, the more ugly he found it. It was probably a very lovely door, to go with the rest of the mansion, but at this moment he absolutely hated it because it stood between him and possible answers. He listened hard. Heard Joe and Frank barking out updates as they progressed through the house. Front door breached. Joe had clearly busted it in based on the sounds he heard. More noise. More static. More updates. Back door breached and broken by Frank. Outsides into the middle. Gabriel could hear the adrenaline and stress in their voices. They were on point and the pressure was on them. They were running on fumes and the high from the stress they were under.

Gabriel felt useless just standing outside. Just watching a fucking door. Even though he knew it had to be like this it didn't mean he had to like it. He just wanted to collect his Lillian and then to get the fuck out of this hell hole.

He heard Joe and Frank on the mic again. They had cleared the main floor. Checked and cleared. Meant that no one was there. Good news and bad news. No Lillian and No Lillian. Fuck...where was she? Gabriel felt apprehensive. Liam told Joe and Frank to get to the second floor now,

"Man One and Man Two, cover each other as you move up to the second floor. Be safe. Be careful. But for God's sakes move fast! Now!" For good measure he added again, "And for God's sakes don't shoot each other!"

All Gabriel could hear through his headphones was the banging noises of their boots as they went upstairs. Everything was amplified through his headset. The men threw open doors and cleared rooms as they went along. They were painfully methodical. And this mansion was not tiny by any stretch of the imagination. All clear. All clear. All clear. All clear. It was getting on Gabriel's nerves to hear that mantra over and over. He thought they must be almost all the way through the second floor by now. Still, he stood his ground and waited until he had further instructions. He knew they had a process for working through the rooms on the second floor. They'd start on the left and work their way through in a loop, one room at a time. In situations where they had more men, a second team would start on the opposite side and they'd work their way from one end to the other. More "All clears" came through. The thumping and banging sounds continued.

Then Gabriel's heart raced and he felt violently ill as he heard Frank cry out, "Oh my God. No. No. No. FUCK, NO!" Then Gabriel heard him throw up. Gabriel's own stomach threatened to let loose. And then he heard Joe's voice over the headset. Joe. Calm. Hardened. Clearly upset. But still, the most hardened of the entire crew. Understandably so. Joe was definitely in control up there and blocking out what personal feelings he might have about what he was seeing.

Joe's voice wavered imperceptibly as he spoke, "Liam, we have a huge mess up here. The second floor is clear of attackers. I suggest you put Gabe on watch by the basement door until we can clear down there. Gabriel, I know you can hear me. Don't come upstairs. Please, my friend, let's do this in the proper order. Let's do it by the book. I know you want answers. But let's deal with this together once we fully clear the whole house. Please my friend, listen to me. Just hang on. Liam, I'm going to head to the basement with Frank now to clear that space. Gabe...hang on…sit tight. I know what you're going through. And you know that I know. Frank, grab your balls and stop puking. Man up. Let's go."

Liam replied with a strong and steady voice, "Joe, you and Frank are good to clear the basement. Gabriel, stand guard outside the basement door and keep watch on the other entryways as best as you can. I'm doing my best to watch the outside from here, but I don't have line of sight to every side of this place. We don't know if there are others trying to get in the front, side, or back. Watch your back and watch for Joe and Frank too. You know how to do this. And DO NOT, and I mean DO NOT move upstairs without my authorization. If you do, my friend, this will be our last ever mission together. And you know I mean what I say. Watch the door until I give you another order. And for fuck's sakes don't shoot each other!"

Gabriel's knees buckled and threatened to give out as he ran into the mansion. A part of him wanted to run away. He was afraid. Sick. Mostly afraid though. What would this night bring? What would he find?

He thought about his beautiful Lillian. Was this the end of the road? Or was it a reset? Dear Lord, how could this be raining down on him? All he wanted was peace and a solid family. He hadn't done anything seriously wrong to anyone in his entire life. Why did the Lord believe he deserved this now?

Gabriel recalled what she had said years ago when he'd first met her. "Gabriel, I need your help." As he reflected on those words he wondered what help he could give her now. Assuming she was here. In some corner, maybe hoping she was not because of what Joe and Frank had seen. He was so conflicted.

"Lord help me," Gabriel thought.

SEVEN

SEVEN YEARS AGO

Gabriel eased back into his chair. Gazed at her curiously and with a level of amazement. What an odd creature she was. He gave her a very hard look. Lillian didn't waver. Her eyes held a steely strength he had not encountered before. Why was she here? What had drawn her to him? What made him her special target?

"What in the world could I possibly help you with? Really?" Gabriel asked. He levelled a look towards Lillian that was hard and gentle at the same time. Questioning. Open but wary. Cautious.

Her steel blue eyes bore into him. Hard. Discerning. Evaluating. Deciding. Assessing.

Lillian took a long and cleansing breath. As she stared hard into his eyes, almost as though she was examining the depths of his soul, she said, "I need your help me to keep my son safe. He's 10 years old and we're starting over. Again. And it's not the first 'again'. But we're tired. I'm tired. We're tired of running. Always looking over our shoulders. Every minute of every day. I want it to stop. We want it to stop. Here and now. And I need your help to get that done for us."

Lillian kept talking. The more she explained and talked, the more passionate she became. The more Gabriel listened and heard, the more ill he became. How could someone do this to a woman and her son? For so many years? This was not something he had ever come across in his life. Nor would he wish it on anyone either. He wondered what side of the bed he had woken up on that morning. Maybe this was just a dream of sorts. A hallucination? Something paranormal? This whole situation was a departure from his normal routine and boring little life. Yowza.

When Lillian finished her harrowing tale, Gabriel fixed a scrutinizing and evaluating gaze upon her and asked one single question after a very long pause.

"Why me?"

"That's a whole other conversation," Lillian said evenly after a short pause of her own. "All I can tell you is that I know it needs to be finished by you and with you. And it needs to be now. I can't answer any more questions because I'm not even sure why I'm here and why it has to be you."

"So will you help me?" she asked.

Those steel blue eyes cut into the core of Gabriel. He sat back further into his chair and expanded his original question. "I still want to know, why me?, but I'll wait until you're ready to explain that to me. What is it that you need me to do for you and your son?" His chair creaked as he rocked. His hands were steady in his lap. And he waited attentively and more than a little anxiously for her answers.

Lillian sat back easily into her chair, relaxing just a little bit more. This was clearly a woman who was very comfortable in her own skin. A confidence that was clear to see. But more than that...a strength that was born out of a hardship that was only discernible if you really looked deeply into those blue eyes that had both a soul and lacked one at the same time. Heaven and Hell. God and the fallen angel all in the same package. Gabriel recognized the dichotomy and struggled with it.

Lillian crossed her legs patiently and gave Gabriel another long hard look. Then she smiled at him. A hard smile. A provocative smile. The smile of an Angel. The smile of a Jezebel. All in one. What a fucking smile that was. It never made it up to her eyes. Fuck, Gabriel thought, I'm done in for now.

Lillian looked up at Gabriel distinctly and leaned forward a little as she said, "Look me up. Not under this name, but under my old persona from years ago. Google should work. The basic information you need is on my card. When you're done checking me out you can call me." Lillian handed him a card with a number on it. "It's a throw-away cell phone so don't bother trying to find me. If you call me and I like what you have to say then I'll tell you where you can have dinner with my son and I. Don't even bother to call me if you decide you don't want to help us. Or if you are undecided, on-the-fence as it were. If I don't hear from you in a week, five days from now actually, we will be gone. You will never find me. We are very much used to finding new places to hang our hats. Safely. We just want this one to be the One, the last one."

With that, Lillian got up out of her chair, straightened her clothes, and fixed yet another steely gaze on Gabriel. She carelessly licked her lips. Gabriel was entranced by her strength, her subtlety, and her combined provocativeness. She was beautiful and strong, yet simultaneously vulnerable and damaged all at the same time.

Gabriel broke out of his reverie when Lillian stuck out her hand and coolly said to him, "I hope you live up to your name. I want to stop running. Call me if you want to help. My old details are on the back of this card like I said. Do your homework. Decide. Five days from now this phone will be buried and never found. Don't you dare try to trace me or locate me. Just call the number if you are going to help me."

Gabriel was struck speechless as he watched her turn and walk towards his office door. He admired her rear view, especially the nice way her jeans hugged her body. He figured her for a runner, given her lean physique. At the last moment, Lillian turned around and fixed another one of her looks on him as she said, "Have a nice day, Gabriel." With a flip of her hair, she turned back around again and she was gone.

The door shut behind her.

Gabriel felt an emptiness in his small office upon her departure. It seemed like she had taken all of the oxygen out of the room with her. His chest felt tight and his heart rate was definitely elevated. He had started to stand for the handshake but had never made it out of his seat fully. Now he just sat and stared at his door. "Wow" was all he could think. Where the hell did this woman come from? Why was she here? Why now? Why him? Yowza! Now what?

He sat quietly in contemplation, his green eyes staring off into the distance at nothing in particular. Finally, he broke out of his reverie, sat up straight and rolled in close to his desk. If he was honest with himself he already knew what he was going to do. In fact, he'd known his answer even as he heard her high heels click on the tile floors going down the hallway from his office and out the front office doors. He knew what he had to do. And he knew unequivocally what he was going to do.

Gabriel started to sign on and access his laptop. Regardless, he still wanted to do his homework and garner as much information as possible.

As he typed and read, he felt an anticipation that he would see her again soon. He wanted to help her. He didn't know how or why. He just knew somehow.

In for a penny, in for a pound as the old saying went.

"Fuck. I'm fucked." He thought to himself. For the first time in his life he truly felt out of his element, but very excited at the same time.

Gabriel sighed as he turned back to his computer and thought, "OK, Let's have a look at her past. The Devil is in the details. Lord help me."

What he read and learned astonished and baffled him.

EIGHT

THAT NIGHT THREE YEARS AGO

Gabriel paced frantically through the kitchen and hallway. His heart was racing. His pupils were dilated. A sour sweat permeated through his clothes. His footsteps echoed loudly on his floor. Where was she? His footsteps and pacing continued. Some footsteps appeared as though they didn't even belong to him, but to his pets. Actually, at this point just Humphrey. He wasn't sure where Bogart was, but felines were notorious for finding warm little hidey-holes to disappear into until they decided they needed food or water or the little box. His Humphrey was apparently worried too. It was unusual for his canine buddy to stick so close to his side unless he had food for the beast.

What the fuck was he supposed to do now? Who the fuck was that guy on the phone? A voice Gabriel did not recognize. Why was he answering Lillian's phone? What was he to her? Gabriel ran his hands through his dark hair. He continued to pace. Tried to think. What to think? What to do? What now? What next?

Gabriel dropped onto the kitchen floor to sit and try to plan his next step. Fuck this. He loved her. What in the Hell was going on? In a rare moment of sanity, Gabriel picked up his cell phone and dialed.

"Hello." A naked answer as a reply. Not unexpected. Gabriel wished for a warmer answer but knew it not be forthcoming. Not from this number. For sure. Dave was a cold cat. At frosty he was at his best.

"Dave. It's Gabriel."

"Hey Gabriel. What's going on? You don't sound like yourself. Is everything ok?" That was about the most polite response that Gabriel could ever expect from Dave.

Nevertheless he was not ready to give anything away so he drew a deep breath and replied, "Yeah, yeah, yeah. Everything's fine." He lied through his teeth. Dave would never ever know. Nor would he care. The man was oblivious to almost everything in life other than maybe where his next burger or junk food meal was going to get delivered from. "I just wanted to know what time Lillian left work today. I have a very special dinner planned for her and I want it to be perfect. I tried her cell phone but I know she doesn't answer when she is driving. Can you help me out here friend, so I don't ruin this dinner? I put a lot of work into it, and, guy-to-guy, you know we just don't usually cook as well as the babes." Gabriel's heart stuck in his throat as he waited for the reply. There was a sick feeling in his stomach but he wasn't going to give in to it. The pause was certifiably pregnant. Gabriel had stopped talking. He didn't want to ramble. He didn't want to tip Dave off at all. So he waited. The silence hurt him. But he waited long moments for Dave to answer. The grandfather clock in the hallway continued to tick loudly. Time was marching on.

After Dave had taken his time, he spoke. "Well, Gabriel, I'm not sure what's going on. Lillian didn't show up for work today. We just assumed she was either sick or had client meetings outside of the office today. Usually she calls in to let us know where she is and what's up, but today she didn't for whatever reason. Mostly everyone's gone home by now, but I can see if anyone here spoke to her today. I'm sure everything is fine. You know how she gets, so involved in her projects, her work. I'm sure everything is fine. She probably just got held up with a client." Gabriel sensed a discomfort from Dave but just chalked it up to the fact that he never called the guy at work. Fuck, he never even socialized with him during the corporate events or quote-unquote the family/social events the company ran.

"Yeah. Thanks Dave. I'm sure that's it. Lillian often gets lost in her work. Please don't bother any of the folks there. They all have their own families and I'm just being a worrywart husband trying to keep a lovely special dinner ready for his hard-working wife." Gabriel tried to put as much light-heartedness into his voice as he could muster. It pained him greatly.

"Sure, Gabriel, no worries. I hope your dinner survives Lillian's lateness today. Have a good one and we'll see you soon."

"Thanks, Dave, for taking my call. You have a good night now."

"Okay, you too. Hope Lillian's not too late for your supper, buddy."

After they said their good-byes and hung up, Gabriel resumed his pacing. He was worried. Distraught. Very worried. Discombobulated. No lights coming down the driveway. No key in the front door. Where the fuck was she? This was so unlike her. And it's not like they had fought recently so she'd just be late on purpose to tick him off too. She should be home by now. Where was she? And why wasn't she close to her own cell phone? Nothing made any sense to him right now.

Gabriel jumped as his cell phone rang.

He looked at the display. Lillian's number. Please, God, let it be that she was just calling him to say she was running late having stopped for gas on the way and that the previous call was just a weird coincidence... some guy that had some fun while she maybe left her phone briefly on a counter somewhere.

"Hello," he answered. Although he tried to be light-hearted in his salutation, there was an underlying sense of fear and trepidation in his heart. It was something he couldn't shake.

Gabriel's world turned a sickening shade of gray as he heard the response. His breath stopped. His vision showed as a totally blurred fog.

He was ill to his core. Lord help me, he prayed. Lucifer come to my rescue if God doesn't show up. Someone please help me. Please help my Lillian. Please, please, please help my family.

Gabriel's world went another shade bleaker when he registered the return volley. Blackness now. Come to me. With that, Gabriel sank back down to the kitchen floor.

NINE

SEVEN YEARS AGO

Gabriel sat back in his chair and contemplated his female visitor. Lillian. What a woman. Interesting. Intriguing. He locked his hands behind his head as he leaned back. His hair was disheveled from his hands repeatedly running though it as he read and learned and understood. He was now in a serious mood. Contemplating. Deliberate. Deep in thought.

All of this was a very serious departure from his daily routine. Gabriel was overwhelmingly fascinated. Who was she? Was he really and truly in a position to help her? And her son? How had this day derailed in such a wild way? He thought about everything she had told him, but more paramount was everything further he had learned about her online. Everything they, she and her son, had gone through. Fuck, almost every other person he knew would have already cashed in their life chips. They would have already been broken. Gabriel wondered if he could really provide safe assurances for Lillian and her little boy. He needed to do some soul searching. And very clearly he needed to do even more internet research. Lillian was more than just a beautiful woman who had wandered into his office today. There was something about her that tugged at him. There was an affinity he just could not explain. But he could not afford to get distracted. At least not on the inside. It was time for more research and an even deeper look.

With a heavy-hearted sigh, Gabriel turned back to his desk. His computer was still running a plethora of searches. It was time to dig further and deeper. Reveal. Look. Inspect. The Devil was in the details. He breathed out a cleansing breath as he typed on. What in the world more would he find out about her? He was tangled in her net but not totally hooked at this point. Yet. Maybe never. Another sigh. "Let's see who she is. Let's see what else I can find out about her."

Mrs. Johnstock checked on him briefly before she left work to go home to Mr. Johnstock. She knew her boss well enough to understand when to leave him be, especially as she saw his fingers fly across his keyboard. She knew when to interrupt him and when not to. She smiled to herself as she thought of the distraction the beautiful woman had brought to her employer. As a wise older woman she knew that there was a huge gap between being alone and being lonely. In Gabriel's case he was alone, but also lonely at the same time. Maybe this woman would break his loneliness. She didn't wear a wedding ring and thus was not likely married. Maybe she could break Gabriel's alone and lonely state. She'd say an extra prayer tonight just to get the message upstairs. She silently and gently closed the office door and left her boss in his reverie. She locked up quietly and went home. Maybe he'd share some details with her at work tomorrow. Her husband should be downstairs now with the car idling at the front of the building. She toddled down the hall to the elevator, definitely ready to call it a day.

TEN

TODAY

The mosquitoes kept buzzing around his head even as he ran to and broke through the side door as instructed by Liam. Gabriel's boots made soft and squishy sucking noises in the soft swampy grass even at this proximity to the house. His ruminations continued as he closed the gap to the door, "Was it her?" Would he finally have closure? Would this nightmare end tonight? Would it be over? Done?

Gabriel's breathing was heavy. His clothes were soaked even more, if that was possible. More than sweat, there was a stink about him that reflected his innermost fears. Not to mention the disgusting smell the jungle had layered on top of that. Yuck. But there was no time for that issue now. There was a very bright light burning in the kitchen. Gabriel could see the light through the glass in the door that separated the kitchen from the side hallway. As he approached he couldn't help but think that the place should have been a whole lot cleaner given how magnificent the mansion was on the outside. Gabriel took stock of the beautiful white cabinets, the stainless steel high end appliances, the gorgeous marble floors. These people clearly had money. And not just a good living. But clearly money to burn. Well, sthe me folks just had horseshoes up their ass in life, he thought to himself. However to keep such a special place in such squalor was beyond him. You could plant him in the worst possible shack on the planet, but within twenty-four hours you could come back and be assured it would be spotless.

From the side hall he walked into the kitchen through that door. Gabriel paused in the splendid kitchen, and then he choked as the stench hit him. It wasn't garbage. Even kitchen garbage in this heat and humidity simply smelled like rot. This was a distinctive smell that you knew in Texas or New York or anywhere else when the sun penetrated and cooked to garbage inside its bag. It stank, but had its own stink for sure. Here, in this place, however, was a different smell. Gabriel was familiar with the scent from previous opps. Opps that hadn't gone so well. This was the sick and sweet smell of human death. Gabriel felt his stomach start to roll yet again. His eyesight wavered. His head felt light. He was dizzy now. "Where were those stairs?" he wondered. "Please don't let me black out. Let me get to closure. Please my Lord. Please. If you have any mercy, then please. Just please."

Almost with a premonition, Liam's voice rang loud and clear through the earpiece. "Gabriel, the basement stairs are just past the kitchen door. Off to your right. Go there. DO NOT go upstairs until we clear the whole house or I will personally come and remove you from this operation. Then you will never know what we found. Suck it up. Follow your orders. NOW!" Liam could be a motherfucker when he was in charge. Gabriel knew this from past operations and was now on the receiving end directly and personally.

Gabriel moved as he was told to. Even more cold sweat drenched his clothes although they were already soaked. All the way down to his socks and underwear. It was to a point where his own shoes were squishing. His stomach rolled so violently again that he was actually grateful he had not eaten any food earlier that day with Joe, Frank, and Liam when they had reviewed the plans for tonight. The other guys had chugged back burgers and fries. No beer. Just ginger ale and water around the crappy motel room table. Clear heads were needed anytime the men rolled on an operation. Liam would not tolerate any departure from that. And he was a hard-ass about that too. Gabriel had been nervous, on edge, and thus did not eat or drink anything except for a few sips of water here and there. They were all tired from their set of plane rides down here. Not to mention the shitty cab ride to the shit-hole hotel they were staying in.

Gabriel was convinced no one in Sao Paulo knew how to drive. The trip from the airport to the crappy motel was rife with honking, hair pin turns, screeching brakes, and a plethora of other annoyances. Even though the experience would have taken half the lives off of any cat, their driver did manage to get them to their flea-bag residence intact. And he wanted a super duper tip for that driving experience. If the men hadn't been so tired, the outcome would have been different. As it was, they all laughed, gave the driver a tip that would likely feed his whole family for a few weeks in this place, and they got checked in.

The rundown hotel did not give any sort of illusion of a trendy, tourist experience anyone would want to select and pay for by choice. The place looked horribly rundown. The team was actually grateful their tetanus shots were all up to date. The paint on the stucco outside was peeling, likely not for the first time in its life. The neon sign outside had seen way better days many many years ago. Where it was supposed to indicate No Vacancy and Motel, so many bulbs were burnt out that it actually spelled out N otel. There was a joke there somewhere. The team was, for the first times in their lives, staying in a Notel.

Humor aside, for these operations, staying close to the underbelly of the local society provided a certain element of anonymity. They were not here to visit the five star restaurants or cultural tourist hot spots.

Liam had made all of their arrangements the same way he always did. Efficiently. High quality fake ID's. And true to form he always managed to source illegal arms for the men on the ground. The communications equipment was pretty top-notch. The runabout gear was no issue. The technology just looked like a couple of laptops and some funky headsets which passed airport security no problem. The machetes they needed to hack through the jungle foliage were bought in an open market just a few minutes away from their slum hotel, the stop and the contacts courtesy of their nice little taxi driver. Same with the concealed combat knives.

Clearly there was no concerted enforcement regarding illegal weapons control in this godforsaken hell hole. But that was all good news for them.

Liam got them all checked in as rapidly as possible. Money talked, and the rest walked. Not to mention that in this pace, cash was king. So Liam worked quickly and efficiently. The rooms were adjoining to ensure they could all cover one another if anything happened or simply congregate to one side if needed. The rooms, however, were way less than desirable or likeable. Even if you were hot to trot, there was not enough alcohol in the world for you to want to bring your date here for a romantic encounter. Yuck. It was possible that even the parking lot was cleaner than being inside the room. Joe and Frank were sharing the third room on the side and made their way over to get settled. Liam always took the middle room so he could communicate, as needed, in either direction. That left Gabriel with the first room. The men would spend the next hour or so getting connected, recharging their equipment, evaluating and prepping their weapons, and, time permitting, getting a little rest after their long journey. Gabriel got himself organized anxiously, had a quick shower with no soap since fragrance was obvious in the wilderness to which they were headed tonight. He did wonder if he was truly any cleaner since the water from the shower head came out in a yellowish-brownish color. It was only about forty-five minutes since they'd settled into their lodgings that the men all congregated into Gabriel's room to finalize the plans for tonight.

Gabriel gave his head a shake and broke his reverie. He had to stay in the here and now. In this stinking mansion.

He moved uneasily through the kitchen and into the other hallway, turning right as Liam had instructed him to. He caught sight of Joe and Frank ahead of him, turning into the stairwell and heading down to clear the basement. Joe fixed a fast, hard and uncomfortable gaze on Gabriel. His eyes had no clues or information for his colleague and friend. Gabriel knew Joe's story. His history. Sometimes wondered if he could handle what Joe had already lived through. And was still living through. But WTF, who was he kidding here? Never in a million fucking years did he think his life would take the turn it had. And this wasn't his virgin voyage into a rat-infested, cockroach-riddled, snake-happy hell hole. There had been several in the last few years. Gabriel wished instead that he could be frolicking on a beautiful white sand beach with his beloved Lillian and her little boy. His little boy now. The youngster had wormed his way into Gabriel's heart. Gabriel couldn't possibly love him any more even if he had been a DNA contributor. His shoulders sagged noticeably and shook a little as he thought about the conversations he and Lillian had after they got hitched. They agreed they wanted a child together. Boy or girl – it didn't matter. Just a child to celebrate their being together. A child conceived and born out of love. A sibling for her little boy so he could be a brother for life and never know what it was like to be an only child. Secretly they both wished for a girl especially after the late pregnancy miscarriage they had suffered through last year. They had asked the hospital and were told the infant they'd lost at around six months was a little girl. Both Gabriel and Lillian shared their devastation and worked together to console one another through the loss. It took even more courage to support the boy who was looking forward to a brother or sister and had to be told that the baby had died. The boy was devastated in a different way, but to the same magnitude he and Lillian were. Once Lillian recovered they had a blast trying to get pregnant again. Lillian was free, trusting, and untethered in their bedroom. She had opened up a whole new world for Gabriel there. And he liked it. He liked it a lot.

Reality kicked back in to his brain again and jolted him to alertness as Frank passed by Gabriel in the semi-dark hallway. Frank looked decidedly green. Sick and sweating. An unhealthy, putrid type of sweat. He wouldn't even meet Gabriel's eyes directly. What the fuck was upstairs? What had he seen? The foul stench was worse here than it had been in the kitchen. Gabriel's mind went wild with possible outcomes. He was starting to get really jittery.

Every muscle and tendon in Gabriel's body was wrought with tension. He was giving off a similar rank and disgusting sweat, although not nearly as bad as Frank's. His clothes were soaked through, still. They'd be ready for the trash when this night was over.

He looked around the fairly massive hallway. It was decorated with some beautiful artwork and spectacular statues. The art looked to be original oils, with gold-leaf custom frames that would have run at least a hundred dollars a foot. The statues were all marble resting on matching pedestals. They were all of gorgeous women in stunning and provocative poses. The floors were not exactly clean, custom, hardwood floors. He guessed that it was a Brazilian hardwood, especially since it was a local species and held up well in this kind of climate. A good cleaning and waxing would restore the lustre to those floors like nobody's business.

With the moonlight penetrating the large, leaded-glass windows of this mansion in front of him, Gabriel's mind wandered back to an earlier time. He called it the "before" time. He held steady, alert, waiting, and listening as he descended into yet another reverie. At least, when his mind wandered, he wouldn't notice the stench surrounding him. Time passed. Slowly. But at least it passed while he did his wool-gathering and waited. It felt like he was always waiting.

ELEVEN

THAT NIGHT, THREE YEARS AGO

After Gabriel answered the call from Lillian's cell phone for the second time that night, with painful, anguish-filled hours in between, and his heart dropped even further down into his soul, he finally broke down and cried. Actually, he sobbed. That man's voice on the phone simply killed him. Having a vice tightened around his entire body would have hurt a lot less. Who was that guy? And how was Lillian connected to him? Did she even know who he was? How did he know who she was? Who was he? How had they crossed paths? And what did he want? From her, from him, from them. Was this just random, or plotted and intended. Gabriel struggled to carve up and invent some answers.

He replayed the conversation in his mind for at least the twentieth time after that man's voice had answered, screaming at him. "Who were you on the phone with? Who the fuck did you call? I told you no cops. I should have told you not to call anyone at all! Whatever that phone call was, to whomever it was, you just fucked up. And I'm telling you that your little call added a whole other layer to this mess. Not to mention that you added a more spectacular world of hurt to her now. Maybe I should keep you on the phone a little longer so you can hear her scream out and you will truly understand, at least audibly, what your little action did. And I want you to wonder just how I knew that you made another phone call. Think on that buddy."

The man chuckled grotesquely. Gabriel froze on the spot where he was. Another rash of a cold sweat took over his entire body. What the hell was going on? He had a great and comfortable life with his beautiful Lillian. And the boy. He had been certain they were all hidden away from her past and safe. Gabriel never would have left her side for a second if he'd thought there was any risk whatsoever. He tried to get his breathing under control, to level out his emotions, to think, to process. WTF!!! As Gabriel fought to bring his common sense to the foreground a little bit, he replied. "I just spoke to her boss. He wanted to know if she was okay since she didn't come in to work today. He called me!" Gabriel lied as effectively as he could. "That's it. Please don't hurt her. I just satisfied her boss's questions and didn't let him know anything. Please believe me! Please don't hurt her! Please! I'm begging you!"

"Well you listen now motherfucker, and you had best listen well." The man sounded very pissed off, but clearly was in the driver's seat and he knew it. More so than Gabriel, across all fronts. "You don't talk to anyone. Not a fucking soul. If your phone rings and it's someone other than me, you just hang up. If they keep calling tell them you're busy and can't talk. Believe me that I'll know what you say. You go and sit down. Eat your fucking lovely special candle light dinner." Another sinister chuckle. It was a sound Gabriel was beginning to hate. "Want to know how I know about that too? Your little dinner plans. Think on that while you eat. Choke down on that lovely meal while you wonder how this pretty little Lillian is doing. Whether she's eaten all day. Whether she'll eat again anytime soon. Maybe she won't even be able to eat for some reason. Think about that while you chew and swallow. And then think on it some more when you wash up. Then get yourself ready for bed. Maybe watch a little TV to get your mind off of everything. I guarantee that you will wake up during the darkness of morning, sick to your stomach with the wondering and worry. But then you get up. Choke down your breakfast. Brush your teeth. Shower. Shave. Brush your hair. Get dressed. Then head into work like a good little husband worker-bee, greet Mrs. Johnstock, and pretend it is a normal fucking day! And know that at least you sort of will be okay. As for Lillian, I'm not so sure."

A laugh followed a harsh, hacking cough, sounded like a long-time smoker's cough. Then the man spoke again. "You know I'm watching from somewhere, somehow. You fuck this up and then your nightmares can take over trying to figure out how much I will fuck her up. Worse than you can even imagine. Worse than anything you've seen on the news on TV. And if that isn't enough, do you wonder, let me ask, where the boy is right now? "

Gabriel gasped. He just couldn't help himself. The man on the phone laughed loudly and outrageously. "Wait. Don't answer. I heard the hitch in your breath. Shhhhhh. I did promise you some vocals, right? Perhaps not, but I'll let you have them anyways. Why don't I let you hear some from Lillian again now? Just before we hang up again. Are you ready, big man? Best be sure. This is not for the faint of heart. Ready or not, here she is! Drum roll please!"

Gabriel was rock still where he was. His heart was stopped and in his throat at the same time. His chest felt so tight. He couldn't even breathe. He was cold and dizzy and sweating all at the same time. What the fuck was going on? How had this beautiful life taken such a wrong sick turn? He couldn't fathom it. How could his world take such a brutal, disrupted twist within a few short hours? Not even a day. Lord help me, he thought, and not for the first time that day.

Gabriel started to shake and convulse as he heard a hard slap over the phone. His hands went back to his head and clawed at his dark hair. Then that mean man's voice with the same underlying chuckle said, "Go on Miss Lillian. Say hello to your beloved husband. Or maybe this will be goodbye? Talk bitch! Say hello! This may very well be the last time he hears your sweet little voice. Talk!!!" Then another slap or hit, Gabriel didn't know, couldn't tell, didn't even really want to know. Faintly, he heard her small very tired voice. The voice that belonged to his precious Lillian. "Baby, I'm here. I love you." Then she started to sob. Deep, soulful cries from far within. Gabriel's heart simply shattered at the sounds coming over the phone line. He felt so incapable because he couldn't do anything to save his love from this torture.

"That's enough Bitch! Now, how about a little scream for your darling Gabriel before we hang up?" It was obvious the other man was really enjoying this whole experience.

The man's chuckle was one that Gabriel would not forget for as long as he lived. The man was clearly having some fun here. His blood ran cold as he heard something mechanical in the background. Crunching? Sawing? Definitely not pounding. Crushing? He just couldn't process it. Then came the blood-curdling scream that took away all life, heartbeat, breathing, normal bodily function that Gabriel possessed. He'd never heard something so horrible in his entire life. And he would remember that sound for as long as he lived. Right now, as sinful as his wish was, he cursed God, the saints, the angels, and the demons. Gabriel wanted to die. Just fall down and die.

Before Lillian's scream ended, Gabriel heard that sick fucking laugh yet again. "Goodbye chump. Sleep well. Sweet dreams!"

Then the phone clicked. Then hummed. Gabriel sank further to the floor. Held his head in his hands. Cried out from a place so deep and dark within him, from his soul, a place he never even knew existed until today. His beautiful Lillian sounded in such agony and he was helpless to fix it right now. He just didn't know how.

What the fuck was going on? What the hell had happened? What would he do? What could he do? Now what? Oh my God, now what?

Now what?

Gabriel collapsed on his kitchen floor and just started sobbing again. Humphrey wandered over, whined a little, and licked his master's tears off of the floor, then off of Gabriel's face. As his master wore himself out in his grief, his faithful dog crouched closely beside him. The canine sensed Gabriel's grief. After a little while, Gabriel's arm reached over the dog and brought him closer. For a long time, the two of them just lay there together.

TWELVE

SEVEN YEARS AGO

Gabriel sat back in his creaky old office chair. He reflected and contemplated, yet again. Hands crossed behind his head, constantly mussing up his dark hair. He'd spent quite a bit of time on this day Googling Lillian's prior persona. It was her for sure. She'd been through more than he could fathom. The more he read, the more he wondered how she could be the person she was, the person she had presented to him after all of that. His impression now was that she was one tough, hard-assed cookie. Beautiful in an unconventional way. Not runway model gorgeous. But a beauty and strength that shone from within. Steely resolve. She had certainly managed to capture his attention and interest in that one short meeting they had had. And, now, after everything he'd learned about her, there was a strange tugging on his heart strings for her. Well, truth be told, not just his heart strings, but also something very alpha male. Dominant. Protective.

He had to sleep on what he would do next. He already had admitted to himself that he would help her. As he swivelled his chair around yet again and then placed his long, crossed legs over towards his desktop, he still contemplated one more question that niggled at him.

"Why me?"

Answers were not forthcoming in any way as the sun set further into the late afternoon/early evening of this day. What a normal day it had started out as. And how the winds of change had shifted. Gabriel did not yet know how much they would continue to shift. It was time for him to go home. Mrs. Johnstock had left for the day quite some time ago. He had heard her check on him and then leave without further adosakes. The janitor and cleaning crew had come and gone as well.

Gabriel had a lot more thinking to do. He also wondered if he would ever know the answer to his question. "Why me?"

His chair continued to creak as he rocked and contemplated this odd situation. It was definitely a weird intrusion into his life.

The sun continued to set further. Night fell.

The day ended.

A while after dark, Gabriel collected himself and his belongings and wound his way home.

THIRTEEN

TODAY

Gabriel repeated those same steps over and over again as he paced outside the basement door in that mansion hallway. A place in the middle of nowhere, the middle of a jungle. He wanted nothing more than to bolt upstairs and get some answers. His heart continued to race, the adrenaline pumping, the questions occupying his mind. But he did not dare move from his assigned position. Not only would Liam have his ass, but Liam would make sure that this was Gabriel's last interaction and operation with Liam's teams. And Liam would ensure Gabriel left with no answers tonight, another form of torture. Liam was one tough mother-fucker. But he was fair. And stuck to his word. And protected the teams with any and every intelligence he could muster. Liam would shut him down and lock him out in no time flat if he disobeyed any command. Gabriel had seen that strength and conviction from Liam before. No matter how devastating to the person, Liam was a no holds barred kind of guy. A man you could trust with your life. A man you could love in some weird fucked up way. A man you respected. End of story. A hard-ass with morals and fortitude. Gabriel had learned some things about Liam's past from the odd morsel the other guys had parceled out over the years, but nothing too concrete. And Liam himself never really talked. It was a part of the man he was. His code. His DNA. Silence was golden for him. No amount of alcohol after any one of the successful or devastating operations could pry that man's tongue loose. At first glance he was a normal, average-looking guy. Fit and healthy, yes. Not obscenely military by any stretch. He knew his skills, knew how to get things done, manage a bunch of hacks trying desperately for personal resolutions. He could teach some martial arts, basics of fighting, management of weapons, conflict handling, etc. What was most interesting to Gabriel was when he took a step back and observed how other people looked at and acted around Liam. Ordinary people on the street seemed to sense Liam's internal resolve and hardness. People that had no idea who he was, and people Liam didn't know. Their first glance would be normal, one of mild interest. Some even friendly, open. Then, the second take would come. A clear indication to be wary of this man. They would move out of his way. Any errant smiles would be gone. Glances would be turned away. Then they'd all walk in another direction, just a little faster. It wasn't that Liam was scary or intimidating in a confrontational way. He was haunted and confident, but most of what the other people would see was a very deep haunting. An evil sense that they wanted to escape from and not know at any cost. What Liam exuded kept so many people at bay. Most people anyways. But when Gabriel connected with Liam those years ago, he knew he needed Liam. Needed him badly and desperately. Knew he needed his unusual skills. Actually, if Gabriel was really honest with himself then unusual was not the right word. Astronauts and morticians had unusual skills and unusual career choices. What Liam did was miles past that. He was well past unusual. He was a deadly force to be reckoned with. Someone you wanted on your side when you needed him. Someone to have your back, no doubt about that in any circumstance. Just don't fuck with him. And don't disobey any of his orders. And, "For God's sakes, don't shoot each other!" A small hint of a smile touched the corners of Gabriel's mouth at that thought.

Gabriel bounced back to tonight, hard and fast. Physically and mentally. Something had shot past him as his mind had wandered. Something too small to be a person, or even a child. Larger than a mouse or rat, although neither would have been a surprise in this fucking country for sure. Gabriel wondered what the heck it was. No matter how curious, he wasn't about to abandon his post or his team to satisfy his own curiosity.

Gabriel refocused on his headset as Joe continued to traverse the basement. Frank was back down there again too. How much time had Gabriel missed during his navel-gazing ruminations? They were still close to the bottom of the stairs, since the mansion was, well, huge. Gabriel just about lost it when he heard Joe speak, "Liam, this is going to take us more than a little time to clear." Joe was gagging. And he was the toughest one of the crew. What on earth was down there to take a man like him and reduce him to that point?

Liam maintained control as he bellowed back in a strong tone, "Joe, Frank, take your time. Do what you need to do. Do what you know how to do. But be careful. Methodical. And most of all, be safe. Gabriel, you stand your ground. I mean it!". No one could manage a team better than Liam and keep everyone in their place, no matter what the situation was. They all listened to him, to a T.

Gabriel shook even harder as he stood his ground. He could hear sounds from Joe and Frank that would never leave his recollections. For as long as he lived. Waiting and not knowing what they knew was so terribly hard for Gabriel. He thought, again, "Lord, help me be strong. Help my darling Lillian and the boy. Please help. Please, I beg of you."

Time passed ever so slowly.

FOURTEEN

THAT NIGHT THREE YEARS AGO

It took a long time for Gabriel to pick himself up off of the kitchen floor. The cold tiles. A bad breath blew across his face. Aches all over his body from where he had been laying for quite some time. But ultimately it was the constant head-butts from their lynx-point Siamese cat that finally rousted him. Raspy-tongued and determined bastard that he was. No mercy there, but what else would you expect from a cat? They wanted and loved you when you ignored them, and they turned their little noses up at you when you wanted to snuggle and love them. In some ways they were worse than women. Both were felines in some sense or another, but generally, no man understood either breed. They both vexed the human male. Probably a few other species along the way too.

They'd had Bogart for a few years now. He was a rescue cat, bit the worse for wear, but beautiful and well worth the aggravation he caused them. Bogart had his own mind for sure. Got his own way most of the time too! Then he'd suck you in to be his sucker when you least expected it. You'd be comfy-cozy on the couch and Bogart would appear out of nowhere, assuming he'd been recently fed and there wasn't a sunnier spot to languish in anywhere else in the house, Bogart would jump up on your chest, snuggle in, purr a lot to get some ear-petting going, and, if he was really happy, he'd lick your face or whatever as if you were his kitten and he was washing you. Eccentric cat, thought Gabriel. That cat chased everything in sight too. Probably what kept him so lean. And give him cat nip, brother, look out! He went nuts. If his claws hadn't been clipped before they got him, man, oh, man, would their hardwood floors be destroyed by now. That cat could run faster than a speeding bullet. And jump? Wow, could he ever! Gabriel and Lillian had to secure all of the taller furniture so Bogart wouldn't cause it to fall when he leaped from one perch to another. That cat was crazy. Bogart could have easily been the main attraction at a circus. But he wasn't. He was home now with Gabriel and Lillian. His antics in the house were fun. If he wanted out, he was on a leash (hated it, but what can you do if you want to go outside and get some sunshine and fresh air?)

As Gabriel broke out of his reverie, he contemplated that Bogart's scars from his life "before" Gabriel and Lillian were very deep and on the inside. Just like his Lillian.

Bogart had grown into their little family after his adoption from the shelter. Somehow Bogart was more like a dog than a cat. Sure, he had that aloof personality, especially when he wanted, like when he prowled and patrolled their house like he was the alpha-whatever. He did this regularly, patiently, protectively. Bogart would immediately hiss loudly at anyone he didn't trust. And best of luck to anyone on the receiving end of that! That cat could bite!

Bogart's coat was a glossy, white-grey colour. He had the distinctive pedigreed "M" in black on his forehead. Many people accused him of being a mini-tiger. But Bogart definitely knew he was a lynx-point, a special breed, and took full advantage of his pedigree.

Bogart also always knew when something was off with one of them. If you were sick, he'd snuggle up in bed with you. Even go so far as to sneak over and lap up some of your ginger ale when he was thirsty and you weren't looking. Or at least thought you weren't looking. Or, if you were really sad and crying, he'd jump on your lap or your desk and just start to cat-lick your face with that raspy tongue that could hurt you if he did it for long enough. Then you'd have no choice but to laugh, which would result in the stopping of your tears and crying and sadness. At other times, when it was lounge-lizard time, Bogart would be the first one to leap up and settle himself on your chest and stretch out like he owned the place. Which he did. Didn't matter that Bogart weighed over twenty pounds. And that you couldn't breathe properly anymore. At the end of the day, Bogart loved every human in his family. And, conversely, everyone in the family loved Bogart. Immensely.

Gabriel sobbed into Bogart's soft fur as he rolled over. His sobs were so deep and heartfelt that Bogart stiffened his little body. He knew things were wrong and he knew it was really bad. In his own, smart kitty-cat way. His Gabriel pleaded with him, "What do we do now Bogart? What do we do next? How do we get our family home ASAP? Please...if you have any supernatural cat skills, please use them now. We both want our family back home."

Gabriel struggled to raise himself to a seated position. The room swam around his head for a while, but he kept on breathing as best he could. Gabriel struggled to keep his head and figure out what he should do next. As he contemplated and thought things through, his vision cleared a bit. Same kitchen, same Bogart. Yet no Lillian. No family.

He groaned as he got to his feet. What the fuck was he going to do now?

Then his stomach dropped yet again once he was upright. The phone was ringing. "Now what? Who? Why? " Bogart had fallen to the floor unceremoniously. The phone kept ringing. Gabriel glanced over to the phone display and, through his befuddled mind, saw that it was not Lillian's number. Yet, he didn't dare answer. If that creep on the phone knew that Gabriel had made the call to Lillian's boss Dave earlier then would he know if Gabriel answered this call as well? Gabriel couldn't take the chance. So, as much as it pained him, he let the phone keep ringing. And it did. Long enough to make him crazy enough to want to pick it up. But it did. And he didn't.

It couldn't have been more than five minutes now. Bogart was still down by his feet. His fur was wet, soaked actually, from Gabriel's tears.

Gabriel picked that cat up and hugged that soaking-wet and purring kitty. Almost for dear life. Literally. He sighed heavily. Then froze. Chilled to the bone. Rigid. His doorbell was ringing. Bogart growled loudly.

Now what? What next? What to do?

The doorbell continued to chime.

Time to make a decision. The man on the phone had said no calls. Gabriel couldn't control who came to the door. What would he do? He sucked in a deep breath and walked towards the front door.

The time of reckoning is a difficult time.

FIFTEEN

SEVEN YEARS AGO

"Lillian. Good morning, it's Gabriel. How are you?" Gabriel felt like a school boy with his first crush making this call. He shouldn't...he was a grown man for crying out loud. His palms shouldn't be sweaty. His heart should not be racing. And he should sound like a confident man in charge of his own cohunes. But clearly this was not the case here. Duhh. He ran his fingers through his dark for the umpteenth time. Then, trying to be cool, although no one could see him, he sat back in his chair a little further. Then he contemplated his hair in the mirror across the office space. He figured it was getting greyer by the minute these days. His thoughts ran to salt and pepper hair. And then he hoped it would be pleasant for Lillian. If not, he'd dye it. Gosh, he really was acting and thinking like a school boy. Wow. This may very well be the stupidest decision he had ever made in his entire life. But done was done.

Gabriel spoke firmly after their initial salutations. "I'm going to help you. But I don't know what you need. And I don't know why you picked me." Gabriel's heart was racing out of control. He liked her. He liked her a lot. Felt aligned with her somehow. From somewhere deep inside of him he felt like he wanted to be her protector. Weird. It wasn't like him to be a superhero to a damsel in distress. But then again, this didn't appear to be just any damsel. Gabriel sighed again and awaited her sweet voice on the other end of the phone.

"Thank you Gabriel. I know I picked the right man." Lillian's voice was strong, cool and in control. It unnerved him a little bit that she sounded so confident. Did she really need him after all? Was she playing him? He wasn't sure. Here he was, a total mess, and there she was, calm cool and collected. How the fuck was that supposed to work? She remained cool as she suggested a follow up meeting, "Gabriel, let's meet and talk some more over dinner. How about Milestones? It's not far from your office. Say 6:30 tomorrow night?"

Gabriel's treasured jewels were clearly not in his own possession as he muttered out, "Sure. I'll see you there tomorrow night."

In response, Lillian produced one of her signature laughs and said, "I'll be the one in the red dress." Another little Lillian laugh and then she hung up.

Gabriel stared at his phone for a while. He waited for his breathing to settle. And for his heart rate to return to normal. Not much he could do about the adolescent-like sweating he was experiencing, other than change his clothes after a shower once he got home. Wow. He was nervous, and afraid, and excited all at the same time. He guessed he was finally, for the first time in his life, experiencing those proverbial butterflies. His heart rate refused to return to a normal rate again. Gabriel was clearly aroused at the thought of seeing this beautiful and deeply mysterious woman again. He was intrigued. Why was she so troubled? He knew some of the answers to that but couldn't help but think there was more than what he'd unearthed online. Why did she pick him? What did she want from him? What did she need from him? So many questions. And so few answers.

He returned to his baser instincts. He was definitely in need of a cold shower. Likely more than two before dinner tomorrow night. This woman was tightly wrapped, but even more so, he was very tightly wrapped around her intrigue.

Gabriel continued to run his fingers through his dark hair as his brain churned. "Guess I'll see what tomorrow brings."

With an extended hesitation, Gabriel reluctantly went back to his work. After all, the man needed to make a living.

He never fully got Lillian out of his head for the rest of the work day. And even beyond that. He was intrigued. Enchanted. Perhaps even bewitched.

Interesting. Compelling. Frightening (now why was that in his head....hmmmm).

Tomorrow night.

Let's see. Bring it on.

SIXTEEN

TONIGHT

Gabriel heard both Joe and Frank mumble obscenities and prayers through their comm devices as they traversed the basement. He struggled to piece together what he heard with what he knew of the layout. Clearly their military-grade boots were landing on a concrete floor down there. He was disturbed to hear their breathing intensify. Gabriel wished he could bolt either upstairs or downstairs, or both at the same time to see what was going on. To see if he was going to get any answers tonight. Just not to be in this suspenseful, horrifying holding pattern yet again. He signed loudly again. Heard their breathing even more loudly through his headset. Then startled as he heard one of the men speak.

It was Joe's voice that came through. "Liam, we're going to need some time to process what's down here. There's nothing alive here in this stupid basement other than really large insects and some vermin I don't even want to try to categorize." Gabriel stood stone still as he listened, wondering what they had found, what they were seeing. He both wanted to know and he didn't want to know. This was an emotional hell for him for sure.

Liam answered with a hard edge to his voice. "Joe, talk to me. What do you need?"

Joe's response sent violent shivers down Gabriel's spine.

"We need one of your special forensics teams, boss. DNA assessments and also a reconstruction specialist." Gabriel knew that the latter was a highly specialized field, but what made it more exclusive was that so few people provided that service. The price was just too high. Loved ones went missing and the tortured families tugged at every possible string for closure. This skull or skeleton might belong to my lost son, daughter, wife, husband, etc. The few experts in the field combined science and art in their reconstructions. They attempted to rebuild remnant bones into what these people might have looked like in life, before they died, before they met their Maker. Those specialists needed rest after every reconstruction. They put their souls into their work. Gabriel often wondered if they in fact communed with the dead in order to get all of the details close to perfect. When he'd met them, they seemed like angel-ghosts to him. Tight as a wire. At the end of a job, they were thin, bordering on emancipation. But a joy you couldn't put a price tag on when they brought closure to a family member. They all wanted closure. And, heart-wrenchingly, sometimes the reconstructions alone were not enough evidence. DNA tests, where possible, provided origin information. Post mortem bone analysis was used to directionally establish age and gender. Worst of all, the detailed study revealed a blueprint of the often severe injuries inflicted on that body, suggesting all sorts of suffering. Those bones sometimes told stories of years of malnutrition, starvation, and very violent abuse.

Gabriel wanted his own closure. Except he wanted a different kind of closure. He wanted his Lillian back alive. He wanted his family. His stomach rolled again. Then his body started to shake. Again. How many times could he go through this, he wondered? Where was his limit? He felt down to his soul that tonight's nightmare would either end well, or end soon and not so well. He sighed heavily. Again. As he refocused, he heard Liam's voice in response, "Okay Joe. I'll get those specialists we need. But you know that's going to take time. If the basement is clear then please head back to where Gabriel is and wait for my next instructions. And for God's sake, make sure you take Frank out of there with you! And, do I need to say it again? For fuck's sakes don't shoot each other!"

Joe chuckled, a little sickly, but trying to make the best of where they were and what they were doing, "Sure, Liam, I'll hold hands with Frank and sing Koombiah as we climb the stairs. Over and out, boss."

Gabriel waited in fear and trepidation as he heard his colleagues make their way back upstairs to the main floor. To him. What could they tell him? What would they tell him? He just kept thinking to himself, based on past opps, "This cannot be good. This is not good at all." His heart seemed to stop and he couldn't catch his breath as he looked upon Joe and Frank's faces as they emerged from the basement. They both looked very white, pasty. And these were hardened men. Joe even more than Frank.

Gabriel held his breath when he heard Liam's voice, strong and steady, as the men emerged. "Guys, Tell me what you have."

"Boss, we're both out of the cellar now and we are here with Gabriel. At this point we need to figure out what we have, where we are at and where we go from here. And how much does Gabriel participate at this point?"

"Boss, what's next?" Joe asked.

Liam's response was not what any one of them would have expected. His voice was tight.

"We have company coming in. About ten minutes out. Now, you all know this is a private road. Frank, I need you to monitor the time for all of us. Frank, guarantee us you are going to watch the clock with me! Joe, I need your help for something even harder. I need you to take charge of Gabriel, because we all know he won't leave until he sees what he needs to see upstairs. But you need to react when either of us call out that it's time to go. We are going to have to keep it tight. And from my spot I know that Gabriel won't leave until he sees for himself what's upstairs. Joe, take him up now. And for God's sakes, when Frank and I call out that it is time to go, then I need you both to get the fuck out of there! You all have your orders. Do what you need to do now. Now! Go!"

All three men responded back their understanding of the orders.

Liam sounded tired. Frustrated. Exhausted. They all felt the same way. They were finished. Not much more time to go. At least for tonight. Maybe. Everything depended on how much time they had to process the place.

The last words they heard from Liam as Joe took Gabriel upstairs were, "I've got watch on the road. Now get upstairs with Gabriel, Joe. Deal with it, and then get the fuck out! Frank, keep watch and watch the time. I need you to be on alert. Men, hurry. I don't know who's here or why."

SEVENTEEN

THAT NIGHT THREE YEARS AGO

Gabriel and Bogart both stared at the front door. The knock was hard and seemed very determined. It froze them both in their tracks. Bogart kept his eyes on Gabriel as if asking, "What are you going to do now?" Gabriel contemplated his decision options. Whichever way he went he wondered if this night could possibly get any worse than it already was.

With both anticipation and trepidation, lots of both as a matter of fact, Gabriel walked toward the large wooden front door. Bogart was right there with him. Eyes peeled. Ears back just enough to show he wasn't sure either. At this juncture, Humphrey was the absent pet. Gabriel wasn't sure where he might have evaporated to since the doorbell usually had him freaking out and right there to lick or pounce on whomever was on the other side. Good thing he didn't know how to unlock and open the door, otherwise burglars would have had a field day already. The house would have been tagged as "easiest to break into". Whoever was there knocked on the front door yet again. Knocked harder. Knocked heavy handed. Gabriel paused. It was time to decide. He halted for an extra moment once the two of them reached the door. Bogart stopped and waited where he was. With a heavy heart and an unresolved sigh, Gabriel reached for the big brass door handle and twisted it.

There were two men standing there whom he did not recognize at all. They looked uncomfortable standing in the heat of the veranda, bathed in the yellow from the front porch light. Bugs abound. Both men looked dark and gloomy and very wilted in the damp southern heat. There was what everyone would have called a pregnant pause as the two strangers stared at the man and his animal.

The one on the left spoke first after a while. He spoke slowly. He sounded very fatigued, as if his entire life had taken a brutal toll on him. He confirmed who Gabriel was. Then he asked if they could please come inside. Gabriel did not invite them in right then, but rather asked who they were. The same man spoke again and said, "Please, let's talk when we get inside. I'd rather not speak out here where we can be overheard or observed. Please sir."

Gabriel reluctantly stood aside to let the men enter but made no allowance to invite them to stand anywhere beyond the front door entryway. Bogart continued his stare and Gabriel could have sworn he growled just a little bit. Odd, since the cat never had done anything like that before. The two men shuffled uneasily and Gabriel's unsettledness compounded.

The man, the one on the left, spoke again after he gently closed the heavy front door behind them.

"Gabriel, we are here about your wife, Lillian. There's been a terrible accident." The man sighed heavily, and then expounded further, "Well maybe not exactly an accident, but rather an incident. I cannot and don't want to say too much at this point, but we need you to come with us please to make a definitive identification of the body. At least what is left of her. Please come with us, quiet and gentle-like. We'll take you there and then bring you back home afterwards. It's the least we can do. Please. Now. Please." It seemed like it was only the man on the left who kept speaking. The other guy was very silent, looking down, head hanging, clearly bothered.

The man continued. "I know this is a shock to you sir, and very unexpected. But we need you to help us so we can help you. I know it all sounds screwed up right now, but it is what it is. Please, sir, just come quietly with us and help us all get to a resolution."

Gabriel's head swam. He felt so incredibly dizzy. Nauseous. So incredibly sick. As the floor came closer to his head, his knees buckled. He heard Bogart growl for real this time. Then Gabriel's world went black.

EIGHTEEN

SEVEN YEARS EARLIER

Gabriel paced back and forth in front of Milestones, seemingly wearing out the pavers in front of the place. He kept checking his appearance in the reflection of the restaurant windows. He thought he looked pretty good for a guy his age. Still had all of his hair. Dark, but more distinctive these days with that bit of grey running through it. Salt and pepper they called it on the TV. But still more pepper than salt for sure. Gabriel ran his hands through said hair. Rugged and handsome if he did say so himself. He had a decent face that showed pretty much all of his emotions if you knew where to look and when to look. He was slightly tanned which was the norm for him these days since he was a man who definitely enjoyed the outdoors. The vim and vigor of the exterior excursions also contributed to his pretty decent physique. Gabriel was not buff or muscle-riddled by any stretch of the imagination, but no one could question that he was a pretty healthy guy.

Gabriel's self-ruminations were interrupted, when, out of the corner of his eye, in the reflection of the restaurant window glass, he spotted a beautiful blonde walking up. High heels. An inherent confidence exuding from her. And a sexy body that stated she clearly worked out regularly. Then there was that red dress. That stunning red dress. No one in the world could ever look better in that dress than she did. Gabriel's breath hitched as he turned around to stare at her and greet her simultaneously.

In his most confident voice he spoke to her, "Lillian, I am so very happy to see you again. Thank you for coming here tonight."

Gabriel extended his hand to her. He tried not to shake but she was so very beautiful to him. He was worried his palm was sweaty, whereas hers was nicely cool to the touch. The kind of touch you wished your mother had for you when you had a bad fever. Cool, dry, comforting, and if it was your mommy full of love too. Lillian did not seem in any way perturbed. She nonchalantly stared straight into his eyes with those gorgeous stunning steel blue eyes that would make the toughest men on this planet go weak in the knees. Her voice struck his as a little breathy as she tugged him a little towards the front door and said, "Come with me Gabriel. Let's go inside. We'll grab a glass of wine and talk a little. Not for too long though, I'm hungry. Then we'll see if you decide to keep staying on for the rest of the evening. Come with me. Walk a little faster, I really am hungry."

Gabriel felt compelled to go inside with her. His head wasn't clear at all. But in he went.

The greeter dude made arrangements to get them to their table. Private, as private as you could get in a place like this. A nondescript waiter brought their requisite water and menus, announced the specials unceremoniously, and advised them he'd be back to take their order shortly.

As Gabriel reflected on this situation, he felt both conflicted and pulled in simultaneously. As he stared into the beautiful face and eyes of this gorgeous creature in front of him across the table he thought to himself, "In for a penny, in for a pound. Time to get on this ride and see where she takes me."

Lillian simply met his look evenly. Nothing to read in that one. She sipped at her water and didn't blink.

NINETEEN

TONIGHT

Joe fixed his brutally hard gaze on Frank yet again, not the first time tonight. "You watch the clock, man, just like Liam said. All of our lives depend on it." Then Joe's look settled on Gabriel. A very long and assessing look. Almost as if he was looking into Gabriel's soul. And maybe he really was. His next words chilled and dismayed Gabriel more than he already was, "Gabriel, what you are going to see in the next few minutes is going to be ugly. Very fucking ugly. Prepare yourself. Man up. Be ready. I need you to stay in control. Buck up. It's not going to be easy. Stay with me. Lean on me. Let's go and get this over with in the short timeframe we have."

Gabriel felt like his heart was just going to surge through his chest. He was nauseous. Still. Again. His thoughts were racing, but his head, thanks to his colleagues, was clear. Sort of. As much as it could be. The he said, "OK, Joe, let's go. I need answers."

As the two men started up the stairs, there was a scurry of movement again at the front of the house. Something was moving down there, larger than a rat, yet smaller than a person. They would figure it out later, assuming they had the time. "Just let it go." Gabriel thought to himself. His silent ruminations continued on as they climbed up the creaky stairs, their boots thudding along the way.

"Joe, I need to see what is awaiting me upstairs. Let me have an answer."

Joe grunted a little and said, "Be careful what you wish for my friend. Tread lightly."

Gabriel's stomach rolled even more. His clothes couldn't be any more sweat-drenched than they already were. What would he find upstairs? Would the answer be a relief or the start of even more pain for him? Time will tell. For certain, Gabriel knew it would not be a good scene to experience.

They were pretty quick getting up the stairs. Joe was in the lead with Gabriel right behind him. Frank was in the corridor below, keeping watch and keeping an eye on the clock. Upstairs, there was a large, wide hallway leading to many rooms on both sides. Joe clearly knew where he was going. A doorway off to the left. The third door. Their boots echoed even more heavily up here as they moved forward. There was a light still on in that room, with the third door. Some of the other rooms were lit up as well, but this one was the brightest and most compelling. It drew them in. All of the doors were still open, like a large yawn in the second floor hallway. Gabriel's heart was still in his throat. It was racing even more now. Faster and faster as they approached that open and bright doorway. Gabriel's mouth was dry and he didn't feel like he could possibly even breathe, his chest was so tight. Gabriel was so close on Joe's heels that the guy complained, "Enough already. We're going to get there soon enough. Do you really have to scrape at my heels now?"

Gabriel muttered an apology and Joe rebutted. The man knew what was about to descend on his colleague, so he caved on the small stuff.

They entered the room. Then Joe moved out of the line of sight. Gabriel gasped and cried all at the same time. "Oh my God. No! Not again!" Was this for real? Was this the end of the road on his journey? Joe's touch was firm but compassionate as he grabbed hold of Gabriel's arm, trying to hold him up and keep him upright.

Gabriel's voice was hoarse as he whispered out, "Lillian? Lillian? Oh my God, Lillian?"

He moved like a robot towards the gruesome scene in front of him in that room with the dim lighting and a stench similar to what he had smelled when he had first walked into that house. He processed the images in front of him. Blonde hair. Red dress. Face down. Body in an unnatural position with the arms and legs akimbo. Flies and other insects were buzzing towards in and around the body, then moving towards the new humans in the room, checking out both Gabriel and Joe as if to see if there was a new source of food now available for them, maybe even a new place to lay their eggs. There was a sick crunching of maggots as those not in transit ate their fill of the clearly dead body.

It took everything for Gabriel not to fall down onto the floor and pull that body into his arms. Hold that broken body. Maybe somehow find a way to merge together with it in horror and just die with it. What destroyed him more than anything was that red dress. Not just any red dress. Her red dress. Lillian's red dress. With that one little piece missing. The tiny little piece that Gabriel still had and held close to him every time he thought of her, really all he had left. The man carried that tiny little piece of red cloth with him everywhere he went. Every day. He touched it and prayed with it every day. No matter what. It was the only piece of her he had left to cling to. Lord help him.

Gabriel continued to struggle as he progressed closer to that broken and destroyed body. He didn't register the blood on the king sized bed by his side, toppled fixtures, jars of unmentionable substances on the credenzas, more signs of violence on the area rugs in the previously posh room.

His stunned experience was interrupted when he heard Joe say, with his hand still on his arm, "Gabriel, don't go any closer. Please."

Gabriel shrugged his hand off. Looked around with a newer set of eyes and proclaimed, tersely, "Joe. I need to know if it is her. I need to know! I have to turn her over. Help me or not. Your call. But do NOT stop me!"

Joe pleaded with him. "Gabriel, don't touch the body. You don't want to see this. Please don't."

Gabriel pushed Joe away even more forcefully this time and that was no easy feat as Joe outmuscled Gabriel multiple times. But situations could cause a man to exude more force than you'd normally expect. Gabriel retorted and said, "Joe. I have to see all of it. I have to see the entire body. You of all people know I have to do this. You know. Now I need to know. I need an answer."

"Gabriel, I don't think you need to do this. The answer isn't coming tonight. Trust me. Believe me. Please come with me downstairs. You heard Liam. We need to get out of here. Come with me." Joe was pleading now.

"Joe, I love you like a brother, but you know I need to do this. I know we have no time, so please don't fight with me. I'm doing this and we'll leave when Frank and Liam tell us to, I promise. Let go of me and let me see what I have to see."

Gabriel pushed past Joe and walked toward that broken, bloody and initially decomposed woman's body on the floor. The buzzing of the flies got louder the closer he got. The maggots were too stupid to have their feast interrupted. They were not going to be disturbed. Gabriel fell to his knees beside the corpse. He braced himself as he poised to turn it over. The stench was now even more sickening and overpowering. Gabriel struggled to keep his gag reflex in control. He struggled to draw as much of a breath as he could and dared to. He reached for the dead body. No gloves on his hands. His fingers were almost gentle in their palpation of the rotting flesh, trying to get a non-disruptive grip. The fingers dug into the now mushy, rotting flesh. He was clearly disturbing some of the maggots now as they got dislodged by the pushing, pulling movement. There was a sick squishing as the body rolled over onto its back.

Gabriel gagged and sobbed simultaneously as he digested the sight in front of him. It was horrific. Brutal. His breathing literally stopped. His vision blurred. Clarity returned a little bit as he heard Frank proclaiming loudly in the background that it was time. Time to go. Time to follow Liam's instructions and get the fuck out of here. Gabriel felt Joe's hands on his shoulders as he tried to pull him up to his feet, pull him away. Suddenly, Gabriel felt something else. A small push against his right leg, near to his calf. Gabriel struggled to keep hold of his vision as he looked down to his lower leg. When he saw what he saw, he choked on the breath he was holding. He just couldn't believe his eyes. It looked like Bogart.

"Bogart? Oh my God, Bogart! Is that really you? What are you doing here? How did you get here? Oh my God, Bogart? Bogart? Bogart!"

Gabriel struggled around and grabbed the feline and pressed him hard to his chest. It must have been Bogart that they saw tonight downstairs. That blur running by. Twice. Gabriel had even more questions now and no time to answer them. The cat struggled as little bit as Gabriel's hold on him was far too tight. But there was no way on God's green earth that Gabriel was letting go. He felt Joe pulling at him again with a stronger force than previously. Trying to get him up and off of his knees. Gabriel struggled upright while clutching Bogart like he was his lifeline. A feline lifeline.

Joe's voice rang through louder this time. "Gabriel, we'll get answers. You know that. But it just isn't going to be right now, not right this moment tonight. We have to leave. You know that. You know the risks we are facing. We have to go. There are externals coming. Liam's told us they're not far off. We don't know how many there are or what kind of arsenal they might have. We have to go. Now!" Joe had gone from asking to demanding. His voice was hard. Firm. In charge and in control.

Gabriel allowed himself to be propelled away from the dead woman's body. In her red dress. With that piece missing. No way in hell was he leaving this hellhole without the cat. Gabriel had missed Bogart and had written him off as gone-for-good. As a passing thought, he wondered what stories that cat could tell if he could actually talk. What had he seen? What had he heard? What had happened? How did he get here? Why was he even here? Gabriel had so many unanswered questions as he allowed Joe to propel him out of that sick mansion and back into that snake-infested midnight black jungle. Frank covered them at the rear as they ran. The three of them, plus Bogart, melded into the jungle darkness. Gabriel was thankful for his team-mates, especially since his head was so incredibly clouded right now.

Gabriel still did not have any clear answers. Now, in sharp contrast, he had even more questions than he'd had earlier tonight.

The jungle darkness continued to close around them as they ran. Bogart glued himself to Gabriel's chest for dear life.

TWENTY
THAT NIGHT THREE YEARS AGO

Gabriel came to. For some reason he was now flat on his back. Hadn't he remembered falling to the floor face-first? As his senses came back he realized his face was wet. Now he thought about those men that came here. Maybe they had splashed water on his face? Then he felt the softness of Bogart's fur under his hands. He was still right there in his arms. Feline aloof. Watching. Waiting. Patient as only that breed can be. Gabriel noticed his tail twitching and that Bogart was still growling under his breath. As Gabriel's senses returned, so did his reality. Then there was a sense of devastation and some sort of foreboding gloom. He knew it was time to suck it up and man up. Deal with this situation in one way or another.

He raised himself up, first to a seating position and then to his feet. Subsequently, he addressed the men in his home. Bogart was still in his arms, alert and mistrusting as only one of his kind could possibly be.

"OK. You're here. It felt like a nightmare but I have a sense it is and it isn't. I don't understand all of this and how it could have happened, what happened, but if you want me to head out with you then let's go. Let's get this ordeal over with so I can say it's not my family and come home and find out they were just surprisingly late today. But...but... before we leave together, I have one question I need you to answer right now. Tell me, was there a child with Lillian? A little boy?"

The men looked at one another curiously and then shrugged. Gabriel did not know what to make of their gestures.

The only man who had spoken to him all night provided an answer, and not one Gabriel wanted to hear. "No, it was just the woman in the incident."

Gabriel didn't know how to digest this new information right now. He felt hollow. Thought to himself, "Where was the boy?" Then he gathered himself into some semblance of a man and told them he was ready to go with them. He told them to wait in their car while he got ready. They left the house, acquiescing. Gabriel gave Bogart another few strokes, wondered where Humphrey was now, and then gathered his coat and galoshes. He made certain the stove and all were turned off. As he put on his shoes at the front door, he looked around at the house and knew that if anything ever happened to his beautiful bride, he'd never be able to live here without her. Never. Ever. Forever.

Numbly, he walked outside. Gabriel wasn't even certain if he locked the door behind himself. Nothing mattered but his beautiful lovely loving wife. He was a basket case. This experience was ethereal. Seemingly, he felt out-of-body as the men led him to their car. He had to sit in the back. Not really comfortable, but that was not of any consequence of him right now. His mouth was dry and pasty. His eyesight waxed and waned. His head swam. His stomach was tight with fear and dread. His bowels felt like they were loose and ready to let go. He thought about his darling Lillian. His beautiful girl. If this was her, then where was the boy? The little fellow he'd taken as his own these past years? He felt like that young fellow was his own son, even though they all knew it wasn't his own blood. Gabriel's thoughts continued to churn through his head. The ride passed in silence except for Gabriel being lost in thought. Before he knew it, it was over. He heard the same man speak again. "We're here at the crash site sir. Please step out of the car now and come with us."

Gabriel complied with the demand put upon him. He felt like he was in a fog as he wandered towards her car. It was just demolished beyond recognition. No one who had been inside that car could have possibly survived. He thought of a woman and a child. But there was no one here. He took in the surroundings. The darkness, the fog, and somehow the total emptiness. There was no human soul here and Gabriel knew that intrinsically. He approached the car very slowly and just knew. The vehicular carnage was significant. It was all over the road, pieces littered everywhere, for many feet around the site. He wondered why there was no other car. Why? How could this happen with just one vehicle? No way. No how. And if there was another car then where was it? Where was the person who drove that car? Why did they leave? What shape were they in? Why did they care so little for another human being that they just left? Didn't even bother to call 911? And did the boy survive? Gabriel gazed across the field on the one side and just wondered if he had seen his mommy dead and just cried over her body and walked away, not knowing what else to do. He was still just a little boy for fuck's sake! Gabriel shivered in the darkness as he looked around. He must have stood there for a good long while. One of the men just lightly touched him on the shoulder and broke him out of his ministrations as he spoke.

"Gabriel, sir, I know this is disturbing. It's hard to see this scene, but we wanted you to confirm this is her car, and just see what we've seen. At this point there is nothing else for you to see here. And, if you could please help us here, then could you please accompany us to the morgue. Please get in the car and drive over there with us. Sir. I'm sorry for your situation. Please come with me."

"I don't understand. Before I leave here I need to know how many bodies were removed? Was there a woman? Was there a young boy? Where is everyone? I see blood but there's no one here. Talk to me! Please!"

The same man spoke yet again, "Sir, I know you're distraught. Right now all we have is a woman who has been removed from the scene. There is no little boy of any size or age. If you tell us that there should have been, then I'll get on the horn right now and we'll get a search team going. No problem. So, is this her car and should there have been a little boy with her?"

"Yes. It is her car. And Yes. Our little boy would have been in the car with her."

The man signaled to his partner who walked back to the police car. Walkie talkie noises ensued. They sounded garbled to pretty much every human on the planet, regardless of circumstances.

After some discussion, the guys figured it was time to take Gabriel to the morgue to at least ID the body they had. Gabriel felt utterly surreal as he left the crash scene and was guided back to their car. The next stage of the ride passed in silence. Gabriel watched the trees go by in the darkness on the highway. It wasn't long before the car pulled past town and then into the morgue parking lot. Thankfully the lot was pretty much empty. Guess many people didn't visit the morgue during the middle of the night.

In a daze, Gabriel assessed his surroundings as he staggered out of the car. The car door squeaked as he opened it and stepped out and then shoved it closed. The pavement of the parking lot was damp, either from a light rain or just this fucking humidity. There was steam coming off of it. He didn't know which it was, nor did he really care at this point. Gabriel didn't think he could possibly feel any sicker than he did right now. All that registered with him was that at this moment he was standing in the parking lot of a freaking morgue. This was surreal. He closed his eyes for a moment and prayed. Dear God, if this is some kind of a nightmare and I'm home in my bed with my family actually safe and sound, then please, please, please let me wake up now. Please. His prayer was not answered positively from God as he stood there and was encouraged to move forward into the building by the men on either side of him.

The entrance doors were an opaque glass with the sensors causing them to slide open once triggered by a camera above. Then there was a hollow swishing sound, like a vacuum that had lost its lust for life. Suck. Open. Suck. Close. The fluorescent lights were blinding once they all got inside. And it was cold. Very fucking cold. There was an old black man sitting behind a desk, all of which (the man and the desk) was behind really thick glass. Probably bullet-proof. Clearly the local law and order was fucking stupid because, really, who would want to break in here?

Not to mention, what the fuck would they even want to steal? A body? Those fucking fluorescent lights? Hummm, maybe the black 90 year old wannabe? Uhhh, no. Not so much.

Gabriel broke out of his surreal reverie and reflections at the same guy spoke to him again (he'd missed the into/invite the first time). It did make Gabriel wonder if the old black guy was mute. Without any intervention or comment from him, they cleared past the old black guy pretending to be security, likely looking for just his old age security pay and wanting his sentence in this cold, dead place to be over so he could sit quietly in his own home, have a few shots every night, a nice dinner with his equally ancient but hopefully better looking wife, and then just succumb to sleep. Preferably one with no nightmares or dreams connected in any way to dead people. The corridors they entered and started to walk through were stark and painfully white.

The guy who brought Gabriel here repeated, "Sir. Please stay with me on this. She is in private room number 3. When we walk in you will see her entirely covered by a sheet. I need you to know it's going to be even colder in the room than it is here in the hallway. I'm not going to explain why. Your guess will likely be correct enough. If everything so far tonight has been difficult, within the next few minutes, it is going to be even harder. I'm going to be right by your side. We need you to identify her as quickly as possible. Look at her as little as possible. Ignore, as much as you can, any trauma or injuries you might happen to see. Once you're done, my partner and I will get you back home as quickly as possible and we'll deal with what we need to deal with together."

This guy had clearly given this same fucking speech many times in his fucking illustrious life. It didn't mean he was insensitive. Just meant he was hardened to this reality and probably more accurately this finality for the people he dealt with, living and dead alike.

Gabriel thought about the word "home" as he digested this experience. He internalized his reaction, "What the fuck did home mean without Lillian?" His next contemplation came back to an earlier question he had had. Where was the boy? He was numb and his feet felt like lead as he walked through Door Number Three. If only this was "The Price is Right". He could pick a door. Worst case everyone could laugh at him. Best case, everyone would clap and he'd go home with a new car or a vacation with all expenses paid to a nice place like Italy or even just a hundred bucks. Why the fuck was this happening to him? The chill in the hallway was bad, but coming in to the room, it was way worse. Gabriel shivered. He shuddered even more noticeably under the harsh bright lights. The sting to his body was harsh. The cold and unforgiving light penetrated his body right now to his very soul. His eyes were drawn unmercifully to the cold, ugly stainless steel gurney in the middle of that godforsaken room. He noticed drawers with doors that lined some of the walls in the room. Some of those drawers had labels. Handwritten by the look of it. More fucking dead people. Gabriel wanted to wake up from this nightmare. He was desperate to wake up. Now, please God, he prayed. Now. Please.

Tears came to his eyes and competed valiantly with the choked sobs coming from deep down inside of him as he approached that gurney and saw what he did. What was surreal for him was not the lifeless body underneath that sheet. Nor the fact that it was unequivocally a female form. What totally derailed Gabriel was the fabric that peaked out underneath the sheet, dangling on one side. A little bit of red dress. He stumbled. Fell to his knees and choked out an inhuman sound as he grabbed at the red fabric. He felt it rip into his hand. He sobbed and cried as he smelled the scent of sweet perfume coming from the material. It was Lillian's distinctive scent. And the fabric was the same color as her red dress. Her smell. Her dress. How on earth could Gabriel possibly bear this? The circumstances? The situation? The loss? How? He felt himself break down on the inside. Gabriel was lost as he felt the hands of the "talking guy" pull him back up to his feet. The man's hands were sure and strong, even warm in this cold fucking dead body meat locker. He kept Gabriel steady as he said, "Let's just do this, fast, and let's get you home."

With that, the man pulled back the sheet just enough to expose only what he needed to. Gabriel directed his gaze to the dead woman's body in the red dress. He simply gasped, "Oh my God." Then his world went black again. For the second time that night.

TWENTY ONE

SEVEN YEARS AGO

The waiter was cordial and handsome in his own quiet way. He was clearly assessing them, likely part of his character and how he landed in this role and made the best tips possible. But he was silent as he delivered their two glasses of Merlot and also deposited the glasses of water and the requisite bread basket. He gave Gabriel a look to indicate he was going to give them some space for a bit before returning to collect their order. Gabriel nodded back in that unspoken guy-language to which women are largely not privy to. As the waiter's footsteps echoed his departure, the struggle between Gabriel and Lillian to initiate or take hold of the conversation was exacerbated. The air was quite heavy between them and made them both a little uncomfortable. He thought she looked so very beautiful. Strong, yet with a frailty that was palpable. A complete juxtaposition all inside of one woman. Hmmm. He guessed that the gorgeous blonde hair was very soft to the touch. As soft as cotton. Moving on to those steel blue eyes that spoke volumes in a single glance. Hard and tender. Again. Mixed messages. She held back to protect what was inside, what was close to her. Gabriel imagined how a man would feel if he could make a woman like her just light up with a smile that came from all the way inside of her. He imagined how that smile would add a glow to her face. How she would just shine. And he knew that if it was him who'd caused it, he'd feel like a million bucks. To see inside of her soul and understand the adversity she'd gone through, at least at this point in his imagination anyways, a complete heart-felt smile would compare to winning a lottery ticket. Something to be cherished. Held onto. Appreciated.

He kept assessing her. Her lips were painted in a pretty pink gloss. Nothing showy. And good Lord, she smelled divine! Then there was the rest of her. Smoking hot body in a classy and exceptional red silk dress. Red hot. Low cut but not inappropriate. Just right. Just so. She clearly understood herself and portrayed it, but didn't flaunt it. He thought she was very sexy. He kept going on his assessment of her. The hemline on her dress was decent. Just around the knee. Not too provocative. At the end of the day, he thought, "She's strong, beautiful, confident, and sexy." I could, and have done, significantly worse. But not tonight. And that red silk dress, he thought to himself, "Wow. It suits her!"

She gently cleared her throat to break him out of his analysis. A woman like her knew when she was being given the "once over" by a man, and with her looks, that happened often. They both took a few sips of their wine as they perused the menu. She still hadn't said a word to him. The vigilant waiter came back once their menus were closed. He addressed Lillian first. "Miss, may I please have your order?" Lillian had charmed him at first sight. Gabriel's gut clenched a little bit as he was the jealous type, but also knew that about himself and held back. The waiter was drenched in Lillian's aura (how could he not be?) as she told him she really wanted chicken wings, very piquante, and a Caesar salad. Please and thank you. Gabriel could have been dog meat at this point, but he was not going to let this dude interfere with his evening. The waiter deigned to ask Gabriel what he wanted for dinner. Steak and a salad. Medium rare if possible. Gabriel wondered if the guy was just going to bring him the cow, complete with the bell, and say, "Here. Sir. Does this look like the cow you want to eat? Care to tell her you just want a chunk out of her side for today and she can now go on her merry way?" Gabriel shook his head. His mind was wandering. Silly thoughts abound. If he'd known Lillian better he would have told her his mental ramblings and they could have shared a laugh or two. But he didn't know her well enough, yet, to try out his oddball wit on her. He gave his head a shake to clear it. Enough was enough. It was time to get a little more serious here.

They both waited in silence until the waiter came back with their salads. Gabriel scarfed down two pieces of bread and pretty much demolished his glass of wine. He then sighed and said calmly, "So. Lillian. What is it that you want from me? Why are we here? Why did you pick me? Why? Why? Why?" Lillian paused for a bit as she reached for some bread herself. She took a nibble and then looked at him thoughtfully.

Gabriel must have been a little louder in his questions than he'd thought because the waiter suddenly appeared again to refresh their basket of bread. Really dude? Not only was that disturbing, but the guy also lingered to make a show of lighting the candles he had ignored before now. Really? The waiter topped up the wine and water and said he would be right back with their dinners. Gabriel thanked him but simultaneously wished him away. He couldn't blame the kid. Who wouldn't want to be around this lovely woman? He returned his gaze to Lillian and waited in a pregnant silence for her response.

She signed before speaking. Thoughtful, with a clear indication of trepidation.

"I want my son to have a sense of normalcy to his life. We've been on the run for so long now. I've home-schooled him as best as I could over the years, but as a result he has no friends and has never attended a single birthday party. I want him to have that. I want him to go to a proper school for the first time in his life. I want him to have some friends. To be settled somewhere. To know he has a home to come to every night and not wonder if we're on the road again. I want him to play baseball, basketball, football, whatever. I want to be able to take him to the supermarket with me and not be afraid to speak his own true name when some nice old lady asks and tells us how adorable he is. I want to stop lying about his age. I just want a normal life for him, and, by extension, for me too. So that's the first part of my answer. My next point is around why I picked you specifically. With your career and long-term residency in this community, you have the credibility to make this happen. To help make us safe and allow us to make an invisible home here. Everyone here will simply believe you regardless of the fact that my son and I are strangers here. But there's more. I've been drawn to you. I know this is going to sound weird, but just let me talk. If you can't handle it, then just get up and walk away. I'll make it on my own."

She took another sip of wine as if to bolster herself a bit. Both of them had managed to scarf down the salads in front of them by now. The main course wouldn't be far off. She cleared her throat again and continued, "I believe you've dug into my past and have some sense of my life up until a few years ago. You need to understand that going through what I've gone through, you either find new ways to survive or you give up and die, sometimes physically and sometimes just mentally, either way, they're the same because you're dead. For me, survival was the only option. I learned to anticipate the actions and responses of the people around me, the people who regularly hurt me. I got to a point where I could read them before they went off and then I changed my demeanor and behavior to squelch their abuse, or at the very least lessen it. As the years went on, I learned how to read other people, strangers, in fact. My skills, if you want to call them that, developed into a predictive sense of some sort. I simply knew when to move, where to stop and settle for a while, whom to trust a little, and when to hit the road again. It's served me well over the last few years. But you must be able to imagine that always being on the lookout and then being ready to grab your stuff and go wears on a person. It wears you down. I'm tired of it. Once I got here, I had a sense that this place could be home for me for more than just a few weeks or months. That it could be permanent. It's the first time I've felt that. When I explored the town and did some research at the local library, I was somehow, oddly, drawn to you. Call it instinct. Call it Divine intervention. Call it whatever you want. I trust myself and I trust what my gut is telling me. So, handsome, here we are."

With that, she sat back in her chair, had another sip of wine and nibbled on her bread a little more.

Gabriel had listened quietly and intently while chowing down on yet another few slices of bread and drinking his second glass of wine. As he digested her words, he also regarded her closely across the table and could not stop himself from thinking about how sexy and beautiful she was. Hot. Definitely not Barbie-style, but really hot nevertheless. Not supermodel-style empty-upstairs in the brain department for sure either. Lillian was stunning in her own unique way. Something about her made his heart beat faster and made his mouth way drier than it should rightfully be. Plus there were a few other tingling side-effects which a proper gentleman would not discuss. Her diatribe intrigued him. He'd never met a woman quite like her. Smart, edgy, sexy, intuitive. Oh, his list could go on and on.

In for a penny, in for a pound.

He held her gaze solidly before answering her, the silence beckoning to be filled.

His response was simple and to the point. "I'm in."

There, the words were out. Spoken out loud. Can't take them back. His heart raced. Her breath hitched. There was a hint of a smile on her lovely face, just a hint though.

"So what do we do next?" he asked.

Almost as if on cue, the annoyingly persistent waiter appeared at their table with his steak and her wings. Gabriel asked the guy to bring them some more wine, although he probably could have just waited since the guy showed up pretty regularly all of his own accord.

Before they dug into their meals, Gabriel cleared his throat and asked her a question. "Please, Lillian, can we say grace together? If you don't want to then that's okay too. I'll just say my own prayer."

Lillian looked a little taken back and maybe just slightly perplexed at his request before she answered his query.

"Well, Gabriel, it's been many years since I spoke to God in any way other than to curse him for my hardships and what my little boy has to keep enduring. My faith got lost by the roadside many years ago and I'd feel like a fool to start now. I do feel like a fool. I always asked God in those earlier days why He did what He did. Why my little boy had to suffer so much. It truly wasn't about me. It was about him. I never got any answers back though, and maybe that's how it's supposed to be. Although maybe I now have an answer in the form of you, and maybe that's what He decided before I quit praying to him. Perhaps you are our guardian angel, Gabriel, so I will bow my head with you and give thanks for that. Please start."

With that, Lillian bowed her head. Clasped her hands together. Closed her eyes. Waited, almost reverently. Gabriel made the sign of the cross and started to thank God for his daily blessings, their food, his current table companion, and then asked for His hand to guide him in this journey he'd now committed to, to help Lillian and her son. When he was finished, he did the sign of the cross again and said, "Amen."

Although she would likely never admit it, Lillian was touched deeply by Gabriel's prayer and how heart-felt and sincere it seemed to be. She repeated her own "Amen" and then said, "This smells wonderful! Let's dig in before it all gets too cold."

She picked up her fork, looked at her wings, gave a shrug, put down the fork and commenced eating with her fingers. The girl clearly had a hearty appetite. Or maybe it was just a habit that you ate fast whenever something decent landed in front of you because you never knew how much time you had to eat or how long you had to wait until the next plate of food presented itself. Gabriel suspected it was more than a little of both situations. He absorbed the moment but his wool-gathering was interrupted by that persistent waiter. Again. This time he brought more wine, which Gabriel reluctantly admitted to himself he had asked for, plus some extra serviettes and an entire pitcher of ice water. Gabriel thanked the guy and hoped that he had enough common sense to now stay away until their plates were ready to be cleared or they seemed in need of more wine.

Their dinner conversation bordered on non-existent at this point. Lillian was clearly focused on demolishing the food in front of her. Gabriel feasted on his steak and admitted to himself that it was rather excellent. It came with a side of mushrooms and a strange deep-fried onion. All good. When they paused eating periodically, their conversation hovered around topics about the weather, how their respective plates of food tasted, what the town was like. Things like that. Nothing serious. Nothing really telling. Just chit-chat. Gabriel reflected that he didn't even know where she and her son hailed from last. He wondered where they were living in town but didn't dare ask because he was afraid it would spook her.

Their dinner was quite good, given that where they were dining was a fairly average chain food restaurant. Plus the plates and cutlery and everything were clean, which mattered to both of them. The waiter, although pesky in Gabriel's slanted opinion, was diligent with his duties. He brought them a third glass of wine as they ate. The extra wine made things a little smoother and easier around the edges. They contemplated dessert as the persistent waiter removed their empty plates.

A comfortable silence permeated their space as they waited for their lattes and dessert. Mixed berries for Lillian and a slice of pecan pie for Gabriel. He noticed again that the woman could eat, but also that she was careful about what she ate. Once dessert was done, which didn't take long at all, especially when she stole a bite of his pie with a little kid kind of smirk, and they lingered over their coffees, the discussion turned back to reality. Lillian started off.

"Gabriel, I'm going to tell you what we need from you. First off, I need a new set of names for my son and I. What I mean by that is that you authenticate something for us. Everyone from the bureaucrats to the lawyers to the clerks all know you and trust you here. You'd just have to tell everyone that you know us and that we lost all of our ID, maybe stolen or in a fire or something like that. I urgently need to settle down with my son and this is the only way I can think to do it. New names, new id's, all in a new town, all with no links to the past. This vagabond life on the run is no way to grow up and learn how to become a normal, proper human being in society." At that point, Lillian paused. Stared at Gabriel with those steel blue eyes of hers. Waited. Another pregnant pause.

Gabriel leaned back in his chair. Stared back at her.

His breathing steadied and then he answered her. "OK. I'm your man. I can do that. Why don't you come by my office first thing Monday morning and we'll get the paperwork rolling? We'll figure out the names and the back-story and all of that. Now I have a request for you."

She looked startled and a little wary. That made him laugh just a little and say, "It's nothing terrible. Don't be afraid. Although these circumstances are highly unusual, I have enjoyed meeting you and spending time with you. Beyond what we're planning to work on together, if you will excuse my forwardness, I would like to see you again. Please."

He saw her shoulders drop a little as she calmed. The slight smile returned to her lips. Her head tilted a bit to one side.

He continued to stay seated back in his chair, uncomfortable as it was now. It felt like the proverbial hot-seat as he waited for her response. Much as he tried, and he knew people, he could not read her expression. Then that damned fucking waiter had to show up, right then and there with the check. The guy's timing was not in sync with Gabriel's for sure. Gabriel gave him a hard and ungrateful look that would have melted ice. Fucking guy. Then told him to get his damn portable credit card machine. Lillian stayed silent the entire time, the hint of laughter moving to her eyes. She finished her coffee. Continued to look at him. She was amused at his agitation. Reflective woman for certain, he thought. Gabriel finished paying the bill and then asked her if he could walk her to her car when she was ready. She answered affirmatively and stood, the most lovely woman in the place. Other diners stopped their conversations to look at this beauty in her red silk dress. They were more than likely wondering what the hell she was doing with him. She was beautiful and he was fairly ordinary, in his own opinion. She collected her things and proceeded to walk out in front of Gabriel. The stares from other people continued and she just kept going, ignoring them all. She didn't care. Clearly. Self-confident. As had happened on the way in, a few other diners recognized Gabriel and said a few words to him. Gabriel laughed to himself at a few of the Nosey Nellies who really wanted to know who he was with, but he ignored them in a gentlemanly fashion.

He followed her out. The door hissed open and shut for them, the cool night air greeting them as they walked out. It was a few degrees cooler than it had been earlier that evening. Lillian's heels clicked as they walked across the pavement to her car. The thing looked like a rental to him, but what did he know? He didn't get out of this town often. Still, it was a car that sort of didn't really belong here and one that didn't really suit her.

She unlocked her door and turned back to him. Her silk dress swished, her pretty blonde hair swayed. All she said was, "Yes."

Gabriel was dumbfounded. "Yes what?"

He was puzzled for a few more seconds. Then she smiled as if she had caught the little boy inside of him.

"Yes. I would like to see you again too Gabriel. How about we talk about it on Monday after we work out the details?"

She surprised him even more when she leaned in and gave him a warm, sweet kiss. On the lips. Not passionate. Not dramatic. But also not the way you'd kiss your grandpa either. Just, well, nice. How was that for a fucking description? I got a nice kiss goodnight. Nice. Nice. Maybe really nice, but still nice. Nice enough to wake up the butterflies in his stomach.

"Thank you for dinner Gabriel. It was a lovely evening and I can't begin to tell you the last time I had such a delightful and peaceful night out." She turned around then and simply got into her car. Gabriel caught a glimpse of her legs underneath as that beautiful red dress rode up a little higher. Very fine looking legs. She closed her door, turned her car on and gave him a little wave as she drove away.

Gabriel just stood there in the parking lot and stared after her. He jammed his hands in his pockets. He felt like he missed her already. He was anxious about seeing her again on Monday. And hopefully many other times. Monday seemed like an eternity away, and yet, somehow, too soon. The dichotomy of the situation didn't escape him.

After a few minutes of reflection, he turned on his heels and walked towards his own car. Then drove home in silence. Home to simply hang out with Humphrey. Gabriel had been alone for many years, but for the first time in his life, he felt lonely.

TWENTY TWO

TONIGHT

They traversed back through the jungle. Thick. Green. Full of humidity. Wet. Insects. Other unknowns that the men didn't even want to know existed on this planet. The sounds were somehow very disturbing to them. Buzzing, slithering, and again, wet. There was less concern about noise on the return trip. Right now it was all about speed and getting out. They'd already breached the property, had gleaned what they could in the short window of time they'd had, so now was all about getting the heck out of Dodge. Mind you, the men weren't stupid about the noise either. They didn't speak. They listened for other people-sounds. They went as fast as they could, safely. They stayed alert. The three men struggled and fought with the foliage to get back to the jeep. Gabriel was in the rear with Bogart. Everyone hoped that the crappy rental piece of shit that would hopefully take them out of here. The insects pretty much ate them all alive on the way. Bogart did the best out of all of them. Lord knew it was pretty difficult to bite through cat fur. After an hour of this battle they finally made it to the shit-box vehicle. The men were relieved to get up and out of the jungle muck and at least put a piece of sheet metal between them and it. Bogart didn't care either way. He was being carried. The guys hoped that nothing had happened to the vehicle and that it'd start.

Joe got behind the wheel. Frank got in shotgun position. Their adrenaline rush was starting to subside. The headlights stayed off on purpose. The shit box started with a few tense hesitations. The next step was to drive carefully given that they knew "visitors" were in the area and that they still had to collect Liam somewhere along the way. Once that happened they needed to find their way back to that shithole hotel from hell. The men stayed silent, each rehashing in his own mind what they'd gone through tonight and what they'd seen.

As Gabriel clutched Bogart to his chest, he choked back tears and sobs, more than just a little bit. The feline was head-butting him like nobody's business. Gabriel wouldn't admit it to any one of the men, there was a rule about male pride after all, but he had truly missed that little creature. Certainly not nearly as much as Lillian and her son, but it was a close comparable. He choked up even further as he pictured Lillian in his mind's eye. Where was she really? What the hell was going on? Had she had the comfort of Bogart for a while? How the hell was he even going to cope with all of this?

His silent musings were interrupted as Joe squashed the silence.

"Frank, I think we're here at the pick-up point. Liam should be here. But we're not taking any chances, so keep your gun locked and loaded while I slow down. Be ready. Keep your eyes open."

Frank grunted his response and Joe knew his team mate was onboard. And on the ready.

The jeep slowed to a stop in the dark and silence permeated the vehicle as the seconds ticked by. The men and the cat and the jeep all waited for Liam. Joe kept time. If Liam didn't come within the next few minutes they all had to just evacuate. With or without him. That was one of the rules in this business, and in this business they all had to live by the rules or risk annihilation. Frank watched the jungle foliage around them anxiously. He was ready to shoot. Joe was ready to drive off. Gabriel hugged the cat like he was a lifeline. Fight or flight. Minutes ticked by. Birds, monkeys, giant insects passed by as the men waited. More seconds and minutes passed. They seemed endless. After what seemed like an eternity, Liam emerged from the jungle forest. The men all sighed with a little bit of relief. He climbed into the back of the jeep with efficiency and confidence before he barked out his orders. That was Liam for you. The man never stopped being boss.

"Let's go team! Drive, Joe! What are you waiting for, a date? Move it!"

Joe grinned and put the jeep into gear and started the drive back to their sleazy hotel.

Liam leaned into Gabriel and asked softly, "How are you doing my friend?"

Gabriel's eyes welled up with tears as he felt the man's compassion for him and it took him a while to answer. "I'm holding on. I need answers, Liam. But there's nothing coming to me. After all of these years. Nothing. There's a hitch at every turn. What am I supposed to do Liam? That woman tonight. It was Lillian's dress but I don't know if it's her. And this cat has gotten me even more confounded. Why is he here? How did he get here? Is it her? Was it her? What am I supposed to do now? What am I supposed to think? What? Liam, what?"

Gabriel continued to stroke Bogart. And the cat continued to purr.

Liam collected his thoughts and took his time to build his answer before verbalizing it. "I get it Gabriel. Of all people you know that I know what you're going through. You know my history. You know the cross I carry. At the end of the day I understand your pain and I understand your need to know. I truly know. I have wondered how many times you can hit that same brick wall and still stay standing. It always seems to be a dead end for you, and I don't mean it like that. It's a dead end from an answers standpoint. And it's even harder when you don't get an answer and when shortly after each one of these missions you get taunted into wondering even more. But there is no option to give up. If you did then you may as well commit suicide because your life would be hell on earth if you gave up the hunt for resolution. And after resolution there might even be another hunt for retribution if life is not restored to a happily ever after. Plus you know if your Lillian was in your shoes, she wouldn't give up either. At the end of this we may well learn that she's tougher then you or I or all of us guys put together. You know she's a fierce fighter. Especially for a woman. Every one of us here is here today to help you because we built this team out of a sick camaraderie around our own perils and demons. We came together because we need each other. Under any sort of normal circumstances none of us would be friends or even acquaintances. Forget being buddies. We're not. Regardless of what happens. Yet here we are. We've got each other's backs and we are a force to be reckoned with."

Liam paused at that point to take a sip of water. This ordeal left him drained on so many fronts. Some of these missions were easy from the standpoint that it was over very quickly. Catch and go home. Catch and go to a funeral. Happiness or grief. Either way, there was an end. This one with Gabriel was taking a long time. And time was taking its toll. He looked over at the man he now considered his ally. Sad that this was how their relationship had been formed. But they were kindreds, none the less.

Gabriel sighed heavily again. Tears kept threatening to cross his lower lids and he contained the sobs waiting to burst out of his chest. He just kept on stroking Bogart. That soft fur. He started to choke and when the tears came tumbling, he buried his face into Bogart's fur to hide them. Then he inhaled that sweet scent of Lillian's perfume. He had no clue how that was even possible. How could this cat smell of Lillian? Was that decomposed body back there really her?

He spoke after a while. "I've got all that Liam. I understand why I'm here. Didn't freak out when I had to leave even though I now have more questions than answers. And don't think for one minute I don't appreciate all you've brought into this relationship or partnership or whatever the fuck you call this thing we're in together. Mostly, I'm under control Liam. I'm keeping my cool as much as I can, probably more so than most men could. I hoped tonight would deliver some answers, but it didn't. At the end of today I have more doubts and questions than you could shake a stick at."

He continued to stroke Bogart's soft fur as the jeep bounced along the rough and uneven road. It was more like an unkempt cow path than a road if you really wanted to know the truth. Bogart started to settle in a little more onto Gabriel's chest. Magically the cat's head found its way into the top part of his shirt. The purring continued, just not as ferociously as before, now more of a gentle hum.

Joe and Frank were painfully silent at the front of the vehicle pretending to be watchful and wary as opposed to listening to Liam and Gabriel's muted conversation in the back. Gabriel knew without a doubt that they had heard every word though. Even then, he knew his other two team mates were on the lookout. On guard. They wouldn't be safe until they'd made it back to the hotel. Actually, Gabriel reflected, they wouldn't have any semblance of safety until they were firmly planted back on American soil.

The deep ruts caused a great deal of bouncing. If the men weren't sore enough and bruised from their mission tonight, then this rough ride back would finish the job.

The drive continued, for now, in silence.

TWENTY THREE

THREE YEARS AGO

Gabriel couldn't believe the sight before his eyes. He blinked several times in the harsh light of the morgue viewing room. How the fuck could he possibly even ever be here? He'd led a normal and quiet life. Didn't cause anyone any issues. No problems beyond the normal boyhood/youth fights. Mostly over clothes and girls and to prove which fellow was the better dude, testosterone and guy-pride as instigators.

What was once a beautiful body with lovely blonde hair was broken beyond repair. Gabriel could smell Lillian's distinctive scent. It was a perfume she always wore. And that same red silk dress. He clutched a fragment of the fabric in his hand like a lifeline. He felt guilty that he hadn't even noticed what Lillian had been wearing when she had left the house that morning. Gabriel started to perspire. He felt weak, nauseous, dizzy, and ill. The bright lights were getting to him. The smell of formaldehyde hung in the cold air of the morgue. All of his thoughts were on his Lillian. He was interrupted by the morgue technician walking in with a swoosh of the almost hermetically sealing sliding doors. It made a sick suctioning sound as it cleared and cordoned off the air, capturing and containing the dead room smells and keeping them away from the rest of the building. It was bad enough that all of those people had to work with dead people all day long, heaven help them if they had to deal with the smell of it too. The attendant donned some heavy duty blue latex gloves as he continued to walk further into the room. They snapped eerily as he put them on. This was all surreal as Gabriel absorbed the entire experience. He couldn't believe he was here. The attendant was not a decently handsome man by normal standards, even without stretching the imagination. He had sick and pale white skin. It was blue underneath his eyes. A sickly pallor. Who in their right mind could possible work in this kind of environment? No one sane for sure. Or if they started sane they sure wouldn't end up that way after a few years. The air exchanger whooshed as Gabriel stared at the man and wondered what kind of a life he had. Who would his friends be? Did they know what he did for a living? Were they okay with all of that? What would they all talk about when they got together? This was all becoming more and more unrealistic for him.

Gabriel shook his head and tried to refocus as the technician turned around. He felt the detective's eyes on him as they watched him watching the scene unfold in front of him. Gabriel's stomach tossed and turned as the attendant spoke, a slow and deliberate drawl with a complete lack of any human emotion.

No diplomacy either.

"I'm going to turn her body over now, put it face up, so you can clearly identify the body. I hope you're ready for this, sir. Trust me, I know this is never easy."

Gabriel nodded at the guy. He shivered in the cold room, his green eyes focused on the body on the table in front of him. His guts felt like they were going to let loose, his belly tightening even further involuntarily. The other men in the room continued their silent watch on him.

The attendant turned over the body as gently as he could but still unceremoniously. Then turned toward Gabriel. All eyes were on him as he cried out.

"Oh my God!"

"Oh my God!"

"Oh dear Lord! NOOOOOO!"

Then, with all of those eyes upon him, Gabriel's world went black yet again today. He fell to his knees and then to the floor with nothing to surround him but blessed silence.

It was not the first time these men had seen a loved one react like that, nor would it be the last. They moved to straighten Gabriel out and the attendant went to a cabinet where they kept the smelling salts.

The air exchanger continued to hum. The morgue clock ticked as loudly as if it was amplified. The rest of the silence was deafening.

TWENTY FOUR
SEVEN YEARS AGO, MONDAY MORNING

It was mid-morning on Monday. A nice bright day by all accounts, although Gabriel really hadn't noticed much of anything about anything. He hadn't been able to concentrate on much in the last few days. His morning at work was nothing short of a disaster. Mrs. Johnstock, who really never even said BOO to anyone she didn't need to speak with actually asked him if he was okay or sick, and if he was sick, she firmly told him he needed to go home and go to bed. Then she stared at him as if trying to assess his status. She was so matronly and caring that it gave Gabriel pause and made him sit back in his chair and chuckle at her antics. The he shook his head as he replied, "No, I'm fine thanks, just a little distracted."

Time seemed to crawl by at a snail's pace. His office clock ticked more loudly than it ever had before. He struggled with every email that came across his screen. He wasn't even sure he was responding properly to any of those either. Gabriel regarded the pictures on his walls as if someone had just hung them up there this morning. He assessed his old creaky office chair. Thought that maybe it was time for a new one, one that didn't creak so annoyingly. Wondered to himself how he had even managed to dress himself first thing in the morning with no help. He gave his head a shake again.

Gabriel had taken an inordinate amount of time to get himself attired this morning. He thought about Humphrey. If that pooch could talk, he'd have all kinds of stories to tell, even if he started today. It was a good thing the canine didn't speak English or human or anything else recognizable. The dog would have by now asked him a bunch of questions. "Why was his walk so short this morning? Why did Gabriel give him the cold shoulder this morning? Why was Gabriel so far away from him this morning? Why was he sad and nervous? What was going on? Especially today???"

Humphrey really was a good boy. He felt a little sad in his little doggy-heart that he couldn't speak clearly with his owner. Especially since Gabriel was clearly so very preoccupied today. The dog took his life in stride every day. And with Gabriel as his master, life was pretty darn good almost every day.

Gabriel recalled rescuing Humphrey a number of years ago. A friend of his was a veterinarian in town and called him one night in desperation. "Dude. I need you. I need your help. I have this beautiful young Doberman. Some asshole dropped him off with my receptionist, told her he'd be right back after he got his wallet from his car. And then just never even came back. Told Annie he'd be back in less than a minute. Listen, dude, this dog is just phenomenal. I have to let you know that he has been abused. I assessed him once I had a moment. He has wounds and scars that have healed on his body, and they indicate to me that he has suffered from long term abuse. However, he is calm and quiet. I think he's somehow resolved that his life is only going to be better from here. You know me, and it's very rare that I get emotional about a beast, but this one is special. I can feel it. I would personally take him home but you know I can't. I have no more room. You know my house is full. Plus my darling wife would absolutely kill me if I came home with another animal. Gabriel, he'd be great for you. He'd keep you company and probably not bother you too much any other time. I'm pleading with you here. This is a special animal my friend. How about a companion in that house of yours?" Jason finally stopped in his diatribe, likely because he'd spoken so fast and now needed to take a breath.

Gabriel had lived for so long all on his own that he couldn't fathom another beating heart in his abode. By the same token, he'd known Jason for such a very long time and had to give his friend some respect on this subject since this was the first time Jason had ever called him to ask him for any sort of favour. Unless it was beer or steaks or burgers or something like that. He knew with certainty that Jason wouldn't be reaching out to him if he wasn't in dire straits.

He let out a heavy sigh before replying. "Ok Jason. But let's start with just a day or two. If this doesn't work out then I need to give him back to you. You are going to have to promise me that if that happens you're going to find him another home. If this is really really serious then you can drop him off to me on your way home. Plus you'd better bring some dog food and whatever other crap the beast needs because I have nothing. And for tomorrow I'm sure I will need a collar and a leash. Fuck, why are you doing this to me? I thought you were my friend! In any event I'm not equipped. And if you're going to drop him on my doorstep then you need to make sure I'm set to look after him decently. Why do I let you sucker me into these things? You are going to owe me big for this my friend! Big time."

He heard Jason chuckle at the other end of the line. He knew that laugh and had heard it many times over the years. "OK, Gabriel. I will be there a little later with this doggy. I really do appreciate your help on this one, friend."

"I'll see you soon Jason. For you, I'll keep a beer on ice for when you get here. No beer for the dog though. Did you both want a steak too?" Gabriel laughed at his own joke. Then he asked, "By the way, what's the mutt's name?"

"I don't know Gabriel. That asshole just walked out on this beautiful animal and we don't even know his name. I just know this beast has suffered for years, bears the scars of abuse, and is both timid and afraid, but also has pride in himself. He's reluctant to be with men, likes women better, but who wouldn't? He comes across as kind and gentle and looking for love and kindness. I think you both will love each other's company.

Give him whatever name you like once you meet him. I'll see you later."
With that, Jason hung up.

Gabriel sighed again as he wondered what the heck he'd gotten himself into. "Fuck, I guess I own a dog now. I really hope he's house trained and that this is not a mistake. I barely have houseplants and now I'm getting an animal. Yowza." He recalled the night Jason came over like it was just days ago. The Doberman was beautiful as advertised. A keeper for sure. He seemed to be a little cowardly as Jason approached the house with him. Likely not his first time going in to a new and strange house. With another new strange owner. As they approached the front door, Gabriel sat down slowly on the top step of his front porch. He held out his hand as the dog got closer.

"Hey boy, come over and say Hi."

It didn't escape Gabriel's attention that the dog shrunk back and got closer to Jason's side as he heard Gabriel speak. He was hesitant, restrained, and hung back even more. Jason tried to egg the Doberman on. Tried to get him onto the front porch. Up the steps.

"Let's go boy. You'll be okay here. You'll be safe here."

Gabriel stretched his hand out toward the dog slowly. He let him sniff his hand and hoped the poor pooch would somehow realize that this was not a hand which would ever abuse him or cause him any pain. The dog had clearly suffered enough abuse. That was evident in his posture and demeanor. Gabriel quietly took in all of the scars visible through his fur. He held back his internal anger. How could anyone do these things to a helpless animal for all intents and purposes? There were knife wounds. Fighting wounds. Disturbingly, there were also cigarette burn injuries. If this dog could speak, what stories would he tell? Very sad ones for certain. The dog got closer by millimetres as he sniffed at Gabriel. Without causing any alarm, Gabriel moved his hand ever so slowly towards the dog's head and neck, to try to stroke him gently. The dog shook from internal tremors as Gabriel touched his fur. Clearly it seemed that almost every human hand that had touched him had caused him pain. The dog's shaking continued. Yet there was some sort of longing that emanated from the beast. Some desire, some hope that maybe now life would be different. That a touch could mean love instead of pain. Gabriel understood this dichotomy of responses, the same one that abuse victims suffered. They were afraid yet they desperately wanted to be loved. They wanted to be touched with a gentle hand, yet they were always on alert, waiting for the hammer to come down, a change of tides that maybe they hadn't even been responsible for causing. One moment it was happiness and love and camaraderie, the next it was abuse and rage and violence. From there it always went towards hurt and pain. It was inevitable. Love, then pain. And maybe after a bit of time, restitution for the pain, not love but emotional bandaging. Until the next time.

"Hey boy, thank you for letting me pet you. Welcome. I don't know what to call you, what your name is, but we're going to start with the name of my favourite movie actor, Humphrey. How do you like that name boy?"

The dog moved ever so cautiously closer to Gabriel as the man spoke to him. A small twig of trust and bonding was starting. The tremors continued, but also seemed to slow a bit. Gabriel noticed the dog's soft brown eyes gazing at him intently. The dog was assessing him further and tried to look into his soul. Gabriel could almost read his mind. "Was this a man who would hurt me too? Or was he a good guy?"

In the meanwhile, Jason backed away slowly. He wanted to leave them alone for a little bit to gel with one another. Plus he needed to get the dog supplies from his car. He stood by his truck and lit up a cigarette as he watched his friend with this poor abused animal. His gut had been right, he contemplated. The dog needed a man that would give him a place in this world where he'd be safe and protected at the same time. And the man needed a beast to keep him company and protect him on a whole other level. Jason knew he was right, patted himself proverbially on the back, and smiled as he smoked and watched the pair across the driveway.

After a while, Gabriel got to his feet ever so slowly. He kept a gentle hand on the dog's fur as he rose to a standing position. The dog backed up a little, very nervous. "It's okay Humphrey. Come inside with me. You're home, boy. I promise no one will hurt you here." With that he held the front door open for the dog. Humphrey looked up at him as if to say, "Is this really my life now? It's just too good to be true. Please don't let me wake up from this doggy dream." His deep brown eyes were full of hope and expectation. Mistrust was still evident. Gabriel repeated himself as he let Humphrey inside. The dog padded tenuously past the porch door.

Gabriel broke his reflective reverie about Humphrey's first day at home when Mrs. Johnstock marched firmly and abruptly into his office. Her tidy little hair bun in place. Those sensible shoes that scrunched efficiently every day as she bustled around him. She cleared her throat before speaking.

"Ms. Lillian Capwell is here to see you for her scheduled appointment."

There was a tone of disapproval that he sensed in her voice, well maybe not disapproval, but some protective sort of hesitation. Gabriel didn't know what to make of it. That wasn't like her. Mrs. Johnstock either liked you or didn't. No middle ground there. He wondered what she didn't like about Ms. Capwell. What had set her off? What gave her pause? Whatever. Gabriel's heart skipped a beat as he thought about Lillian and being able to see her again, spend time in her presence, right now.

"Mrs. Johnstock, please give me five minutes to clear the work on my desk and then send her in. Thank you."

Gabriel leaned back in his chair, ran his fingers through his dark hair for the umpteenth time this morning, and wondered how this meeting would go. Where would their discussion lead them? He simply relaxed and got lost in thought as he waited for the five minutes to pass. After all, that had just been an excuse to Mrs. Johnstock about clearing work off of his desk. He just wanted some time to himself in absolute anticipation of seeing this lovely lady again. He wanted to be calm and ready for her. And, with his male ego firmly rooted, wanted her to wait outside for a few moments.

He sighed semi-contentedly as he listened to his clock tick seconds and then minutes by. He waited calmly and anxiously at the same time. Another sigh passed his lips. He knew Mrs. Johnstock would be one hundred percent prompt. His world was tilted upside down but still right at the same time. He sat, smiled, and waited.

TWENTY FIVE

CURRENT TIME

Bogart continued his soothing and gentle purr as their vehicle bounced along the rough road. It was more like a cow path than a road, actually. Gabriel continued to rub that soft fur while he held back the tears. He certainly couldn't cry in front of the other men. Even though he had witnessed them and others break down, it was always a source of finality that caused them to break, not a source of disparity and questions. He needed to man up and hold his own. The questions he had rang over and over again in his head. Why was Bogart here in this Godforsaken tropical place? Thousands of miles from home. After all this time. Did that mean for sure it was Lillian in that room back there? The rounds of questions continued to volley around in his head.

Liam stayed silent for now, after their initial exchange. Joe and Frank were still on alert, judging by their body postures in the front of the jeep. They were respectfully silent. Of all people, they understood the place he was in. Gabriel was intensely grateful for their total lack of conversation.

Gabriel thought back to the gruesome scene at the mansion. The visions and memories just poured back into his head. He suffered inside as he thought about the red dress. That same red dress. With the patch missing. That same patch. How was that possible? And the scent of Lillian's perfume. He reflected on the smashed head of the body lying face down on the floor. The pretty blonde hair caked with dried blood.

Actually, not just caked, but a whole pool of the stuff around the top of her. Gabriel wasn't even sure there would be enough of her features remaining to identify her even if he had been able to turn her over, that's how badly the back of her head had been smashed in. Even with a gruesome look at the remnants of the body there might be more questions than actual answers.

The team was almost back at the sleazebag motel when Liam piped up again.

"Joe, Frank, I want you to drive in concentric circles around the motel as we get a few blocks out. Let's make sure no one is following us and also make sure there's no one waiting for us as we approach the place."

The jeep wound its way closer and closer to the motel. There was no tail and there was nothing any of them could discern in terms of suspicious hangouts.

Liam spoke again once they hit the parking lot. "Men, I'm going to do some reconnaissance after we get back into this shithole motel and get cleaned up. Let me see what new information I can find about that weird mansion, who owns it, and maybe even who drove up there tonight while we were there. I took some photos of their cars and them as they arrived before I ran out to the jeep and joined you. I need you all to give me some time. Be sure there's nothing else going on tonight. We're parked for today. Maybe early on in the morning, we might have to move, but not right now, not tonight. You'll have to wait for me to let you know what's happening next. Just lay low. Rest. Be quiet."

Liam continued speaking, firmly. "Gabriel, I don't think that cat on your lap is going to be an issue for the resort we're currently staying in. I'm sure the place has more fleas that you could count, more fleas than that cat ever came across in his entire life. Pardon my humour, but I think all of the fleas in that fleabag motel will pounce on your cat in a concerted effort to get the hell out of there, one-way ticket and all." Frank and Joe chuckled at Liam's humour from their places in the front seat.

They were getting ready to exit the jeep when Gabriel's cell phone vibrated in his shirt pocket. He was on a leave from work to be on this mission. His core team was here in the vehicle with him. So, who could this be? He pushed Bogart aside a little to grab his cell phone. He looked at the display. Caller unknown. Felt Liam stare at him when he answered. Felt his mouth go dry and his heart rate speed up as he pressed the answer button.

"Hello." He tried to keep his voice steady and bold, but he wasn't sure that penetrated through the phone line. He put the phone on speaker so the other men could hear. After all, Gabriel had no secrets from anyone on this planet, least of all these guys.

"Well, well well. How's your night going my friend?"

Gabriel knew that voice. He'd heard it many times over the last years. His gut tightened and he clenched his jaw as he replied. "What the fuck do you want? Why are you calling me? Why are you calling me tonight? Answer me before I hang this fucking phone up! Answer me!"

That same distinctive chuckle came back over the phone line. Sick mother fucker.

"I'd suggest you don't hang up now or you'll be really sorry. Besides, I'm enjoying this little game of cat and mouse with you. And, let me guess, wait for it, wait, wait, wait, but I'd wager you have the cat right now don't you?" He chuckled again. Gabriel's heart stopped and raced all at the same time. It felt like it was going to explode right out of his chest. He thought to himself, as he had countless times before, who the fuck was this guy? What was his agenda? What in creation was going on?

The silence in the vehicle as the team waited outside the motel was palpable. Frank, Joe and Liam had tensed up almost as soon as they heard Gabriel speak, then tensed up even more when they heard that other guy's voice.

The chuckle came through again. "What? Nothing to say to me my friend? You know I only stay on the line for a few minutes at most. And you know why. Before I go do you want to hear some more screams? Wonder if they're live or recorded from when I tortured that little woman you looked at tonight with her head bashed in? Oh, by the way did you determine if it was Lillian? Hmmm. Yes or no? Was it her or wasn't it? What's going through your head? Do you think Bogart provided any comfort as she suffered and died? Hmmm. Well, my friend, I gotta go! Sweet dreams. Have a good night and tell your friends I said hello. Oh, and before I forget, make sure you pet that little cat well. He might need some food soon too, unless he licked up some of the blood on the floor, and if he did then he might need a litter box soon." With that final comment, Gabriel's nemesis hung up. Gabriel shivered. He was haunted to the core. What the hell was going on? Where were the answers he sought? Could this possibly get any worse?

Then his phone vibrated again. Same deal. Unknown caller. Gabriel answered. Speaker phone again. He was sick through and through.

"What the fuck do you want from me, you fucking asshole?"

That same sick chuckle.

"And, you are NOT my friend! Never will be. What have you done with my Lillian? And what have you done with our boy?"

"Oh. My friend. And you are my friend. You just don't understand how close we are. You have no idea." The voice was sarcastic. "Listen, *friend*, beyond your cat, I want to know how you liked seeing that pretty red dress again. It was a special red dress for her, wasn't it? Tell me, did it bring back any fond memories of your dates from before? And how about the perfume? Remind you of her? Holding her? Fucking her? Tell me, did you like that touch? Get me off my friend and maybe I'll help you out of this mess. Do you know I am really enjoying this victory over you? It feels so good. Yes, it does. So let's not waste any more time my friend. My time on this call is up. I just wanted to speak to you again. Enjoy your night, and once again, sweet dreams. Think of your Lillian. The boy. The red silk dress with the piece missing. And, while you exhaust your thoughts, keep stroking your little pussycat. Good night *friend!*" Then the sick chuckle as the line went dead.

The men in the jeep stayed silent for several long moments. They were shocked. Their situations didn't involve the same sick kind of fuck that kept calling Gabriel. A different kind of disturbed bastard for sure, but nothing like this. Their enemies had not taunted and tortured nor communicated with them the way this sicko was with Gabriel. Gabriel just sat and stared at his phone. He uttered a guttural cry as he clutched Bogart to his chest. There was this very deep pain inside of him that he was just unable to deal with.

Liam was the one who broke the barrier. He grabbed onto Gabriel's arm tightly and encouraged him to hang on. His words were meant to bring strength and resolve. "Hold tight Gabriel. We don't know anything right now. Just hang on. I'm going to go hunting for answers online once we get inside. If you dig really deep inside of yourself, I'm sure you can call for Lillian and sense if she is still alive and in some way ok. You guys have a soul connection. You need to draw on that. If that was her back at the mansion, then you'd know that too. Dig deep, man, and figure out your part of this. Dig deep and let us all do what we do best. Hang on."

Gabriel shook underneath Liam's touch. Looked at the man's face and understood that demons never truly left. They might diminish or fade, but they never truly went away. Why did this fucking world have to be so full of challenges and sorrow? Before he could voice his questions and go deeper into this particular quagmire, Frank announced, "Welcome home guys. We're back at the minus five star no-tell mo-tel. Let's get inside, clear the rooms, and get cleaned up. Joe and I will go out and scrounge up some chow in a bit. Then we can wait for Liam to get us any new data he finds. Joe, you and I are going in first and we'll give the boys in back the all-clear for them to get comfy too. If you don't see a sign from us in three minutes then head over to that shithole pub three blocks over and we'll find you there as soon as we can. Joe, let's go."

Joe nodded. There was nobody better than him to ensure their safety in this so-called establishment.

Liam couldn't help but get in the last word before they exited the jeep. "Thanks guys. Good plan. But for fuck's sakes don't shoot each other!"

The humorous interjection made all four men smile just a little, even with the seriousness of the situation.

Joe and Frank exited the vehicle quickly and quietly. The team had already disabled all of the interior lights in the jeep as soon as they picked it up. Their guns were drawn and by their sides as they moved forward. Joe had all of their room keys in hand from underneath the seat where they'd stashed them earlier. Frank kept a watchful eye. Both Gabriel and Liam now had their loaded weapons in their laps, ready to go if need be. Hearts were racing as they all watched Joe and Frank enter and go through their rooms. Adrenaline was still at a fairly high level. After what seemed like an eternity, Joe gave them a signal. All clear.

The rest of the bedraggled group exited the jeep, weariness settling in. Bogart, not knowing the situation, was tense again in Gabriel's arms. His alert feline eyes darted around. He had no clue where he was or even why he was here. He was no better off in a lot of ways than Gabriel. His ears continued to twitch as Gabriel carried him across the parking lot while Liam covered him from a few steps back. Frank made his way down to the jeep and parked somewhere more shadowed, more discreet. Bogart knew he wasn't home for sure. Frank watched from way back for a good ten minutes just to be certain no one was lurking and watching and waiting. Then he went up too.

All of the rooms were adjoining with connecting doors. In these operations safety and sanity were both of equal importance to the team. It was paramount. You never knew if there would be an adversary that wanted to mix with any one of them, or if any one of the team would suffer a breakdown depending on what they had seen or heard that day. Better to be very close and deal with things instead of hearing a gunshot go off in the middle of the night and wonder. Or have to deal with another dead body in the morning. Privacy took a back seat often. The men all stumbled and fell into their rooms in a companionable sort of silence. Gabriel continued to nuzzle Bogart's fur as he wandered into his room, almost comatose. Numb. Unsettled. Still. Again. Liam broke the silence once more, reluctantly.

"Hey, Gabriel, my man, let me go have a little bit of fun before I get started on my cyber-digging. I want to launch a proverbial hand grenade underneath that fat fucking woman manning, and I use the term loosely, the front desk. I'm going to incent her, or ignite her, her choice, to get us a kitty carrier, some litter, and some cat food along with whatever bowls she can scrounge. With the prices we're paying in this dump, it's the least she can do unless she wants to watch her fat ass light up like it's Independence Day."

Gabriel understood Liam's attempt at humour. Trying to break him out of his unsettled and disturbed mood. He bowed a little in acknowledgement to Liam. The man was solid and a good friend. But Gabriel was in a really bad place right now.

As the door closed behind him, Liam stood for a moment. He felt for Gabriel. However all of these missions just brought back so many of his own memories, his own pain, and a story that one day should be told. Not now. Someday. Liam tried to shrug the negativity off. Did the best he could. Then started down the stairs to deal with that fat, ugly bitch by the front desk. Now, of all times, he was definitely in the mood for her. Yes. She'd do his bidding. And fast. Or else. Liam sort of hoped she would give him attitude so he could be justified in letting off some steam.

Frank and Joe had entered their rooms, but all of them kept their adjoining doors open. Everyone was keeping an eye on each other. Mostly, right now, it was the team keeping an eye on Gabriel. They all sat up a little straighter as they heard Gabriel's phone go off. He'd taken it off of silent mode after that last call. No need for silence now since they were back here and no longer in the jungle or that Godforsaken mansion. They watched their comrade look at his phone and pale to a sickly shade of white mixed with green. Gabriel registered the display. Unknown caller. Again? Again! What the fuck? Now what?

He wanted with one part of his soul to just crawl into a hole with Bogart and stroke that cat's fur until he died. But he missed his family so much more than the pain he was in. So he answered the call, trying to keep his voice as level as possible.

"Hello."

Gabriel broke down and sank to his knees when he heard what he did. No way was he prepared for this. No fucking way. Did the Lord have no mercy on his soul? Why was this happening? Joe and Frank had come through the rooms and stood in his doorway, looking on in silence. They sensed this was really bad. Worse than the setback at the mansion. Way worse. Compounded past the calls while they were in the jeep. Bogart kept a little distance as he stared at Gabriel after having been unceremoniously dropped. There was no more fur-stroking now. The silence of the other men and the cat was deafening.

"My darling Gabriel. I love you so very much. Please find me and bring me home again. Soon. Please. I need you. I'm begging you please. Help me! Find me!"

"LILLIAN! My God, Lillian! Are you ok? Where are you? I love you. I'm trying to find you. I love you! I love you! I LOVE YOU! Please let me hear your voice again. Lillian. Lillian? LILLIAN?" Gabriel was screaming at the top of his lungs now. The men and the cat just continued to stare at him, on his knees, on the floor.

The next thing Gabriel heard was that same sick chuckle in the background. That asshole was clearly getting off on what was going on. Then he spoke.

"Well. Pal. Friend. Buddy boy. I guess you have some thinking to do. Again, with my sincerest wishes, sweet dreams. Friend." Then the click as the line went dead.

Gabriel was beyond distraught. Inconsolable. He sobbed with bone wrenching grief as he fell further into that disgusting carpeted floor. There were no words to describe how much he wanted to crawl into himself and just escape this place and this situation and this life. Joe and Frank stood rooted where they were, unable to move. They'd had their own pasts to deal with but this situation was a serious mind-fuck for their friend and they weren't able to digest what was going on or how they should best deal with him. So they just stayed put. Stayed still. Kept watch.

The thoughts going through Gabriel's head just confounded him even further. Did that call mean his darling Lillian was still alive? Or was this some sort of hoax from this fucked up stranger whom he didn't know? Had he recorded Lillian's voice over time and that was just a recording? Was Gabriel some sort of a toy to this guy, whoever he was? And where was the boy? Gabriel felt so very lost and so very totally lonely. He missed Lillian like he'd miss his heart if it was gone. Although it was a line from a Tom Cruise movie, it resonated with Gabriel. Lillian completed him. She was his other half. His soul mate. When was this nightmare going to end? Why was this sinister man torturing him?

Bogart had kept his distance but now moved a little closer as he sensed Gabriel's utter and total distress. He simply stopped purring and lodged himself against Gabriel's chest. There was a little comfort in the warm and soft fur against his neck. Not to mention the little bit of cat breath he felt on his skin. Alive. He was alive. Bogart was alive. But was Lillian? Gabriel felt his tears form and slide down his cheeks. He was so exhausted, so distressed, so alone. The old familiar sobs came next. He didn't care anymore if the other men thought he was weak.

Joe and Frank moved quietly into their rooms, still leaving their doors open, but leaving Gabriel and his cat in peace. Well, maybe not in peace, but rather a disconcerting solitude.

Minutes clicked by. Gabriel didn't move from the floor. Bogart would have crawled into his shirt or even into his body if he could have. His fur was wet from Gabriel's tears. They both felt empty in their own unique ways. Time passed. Gabriel had no idea how long he stayed like that.

Ultimately it was Liam who broke into his time and space. He was back from his visit with the fat broad downstairs.

"Get up my soldier. Get the fuck up! You know we have work to do. Let's go. You know how these things go. You can feel sorry for yourself later or never, but not right now. Not on my fucking watch! Get your ass up, man!"

With that, Liam hauled Gabriel up to his feet. Bogart spilled awkwardly to the ugly carpeted floor. The cat glowered at Liam and Liam scowled back at the cat. He shoved Gabriel onto the bed. Then he tossed the cat on top of him. Gabriel glared at Liam and locked the cat into his arms, and continued to sob like a small child. "Lillian, my angel, where are you? What's happened to you? Where is the boy? I miss you so much! I love you so very much! I need you back! Please, God, help me find her and bring her back home again."

Liam decided to let his friend continue to cry out his anguish as he pulled the shabby covers over him on the bed. He made sure Bogart was shoved in there with him. As Liam towered over the two of them, he proclaimed, "Cry it out Gabriel. Just cry it out until there's nothing left. I'm going to give you a little time to do that and once there's nothing left to cry out anymore then I expect you to get up and get on with things. In the meantime, let me do my job. I'll be in the next room but I'll be back over here soon. Get whatever rest you can my friend. I promise you I'll be back when I have something to tell you, when I have some news. "

Liam moved off to the other side of the room to his connecting door. Frank and Joe were silent in their connecting rooms. Sympathy was etched all of their hearts but there was nothing they could do right now except stand guard, take turns with that, and keep the team safe, and wait for Liam to gather more intel. They would need to be ready whenever Liam said they had to go. No matter what they thought of the instructions.

Liam slightly, partially, closed his own door and stood still for a moment. He figured that if cats could cry, Bogart had his own tears pouring out right now. Liam sighed heavily, a huge weight on his chest, a burden any normal man would falter under. Time to suck it up and get to work and do what he did best. Find some answers. As he cracked open his laptop and got connected he just thought to himself, "What a fucking world this is."

TWENTY SIX

THREE YEARS AGO

It was the morgue technician with his little vial of smelling salts that managed to revive Gabriel. Once he came to, several sets of hands helped him upright again, sensitive enough to make sure he wasn't facing the corpse until he at least managed to stand on his own and collect his thoughts.

Gabriel had been so utterly and totally shocked when the technician had turned the body over. That red silk dress was imprinted on his mind. As was her signature scent. He just couldn't believe his eyes. That beautiful hair was caked with dried blood. The arms and legs were battered and bruised beyond anything he could possibly imagine. He wondered how anyone could even endure that level of pain and agony while they were still alive and breathing.

Once he caught his breath, Gabriel turned around again to face this nightmare head-on. His eyes traversed the spectacle in front of him, gut churning. The room was so freaking cold. Drafts of air were coming across his body. How could anyone even work in this place, he wondered? His gaze went back to the body in front of him. No shoes. No stockings. He wondered if anyone had yet checked to see if she had any underwear on. Was it gone? Missing? Had this body been abused well past the physical sense into being raped too? As much as all of this hurt him, his gaze travelled further upwards. There were burn marks on her chest. And lacerations that he didn't even want to think about how they'd gotten there. But it was when Gabriel's review of the body turned towards the face that he lost it. This brought Gabriel to his knees once more. He gagged. He choked. And he cried out even louder. The brutality this woman had endured was etched upon her face. She must be so much more peaceful now that she was dead. At least her pain was over now. The abuse was over for her.

He wondered what kind of monster did something like this to another human person. She had been tortured. That much was clear. Even beyond the bruises Gabriel could see her earlier, pre-death prettiness. But now, oh God, now she was just a sad remnant of the pretty lady she had once been.

The hum of the cooling system in the room kept him levelled. The cool air managed to keep him awake and alert and conscious. He guessed that they pumped all that cold air through the vents not just to keep the smells at bay but also to keep people from passing out or puking. (Good luck with that.)

Gabriel was still on his knees as he grasped at both the cold steel of the gurney and clutched a corner of that red silk dress. A piece of it tore and came off into his hands. There was a cold sweat all over his body. He was hot and sweaty while also being chilled to the core. The morgue room was absolutely freezing cold now. He could smell his own sweat over and above the antiseptic smell of the room. Gabriel brought that small torn off piece of the red silk dress to his face. He could smell Lillian. He exhaled a very heavy sigh as he brought his line of sight up to the other men in the room with him.

He collected himself and stood once more, this time on his own. He steadied himself by holding the rail of the gurney. His voice was hoarse when he finally spoke. His words came out almost as though he was having an out-of-body experience. It was all so surreal. "It's Lillian's dress. I can smell her perfume on it. It's her size and her hair color too." He was choking now, keeping the sobs at bay. Tears rolled down his cheeks.

The men in the room waited anxiously for him to continue.

They were all surprised by what he said to them next.

"This woman looked an awful lot like Lillian, but it's not my Lillian. Thank God, it's not my Lillian! Lord help the man and family that this woman once belonged to. I hope the man she loved doesn't have to go through this experience. I hope no other family member has to look at this poor battered body. But this is, thank the Lord, not my wife. It's not her."

There was a stunned silence in the cold room as everyone digested his revelation and outburst. One of the two men nodded to the morgue technician who, in response, pulled the sheet back over the body. He was slow and methodical, but what else could you possibly expect. The guy was probably doing this every day for minimum wage. The man's shoulders sagged. He had obviously done this many times in his career. How he didn't go home and blow his brains out after any given shift was beyond them. It seemed to take forever as he gradually slid the corpse back into the cold drawer. The man turned his back on them as he first disposed of his gloves and then quietly walked out of the room. His protective booties made a soft scratching and snuffling sound on the tile floor. Like nails on a chalkboard, just different. The other two men held onto Gabriel as they guided him towards the exit door, the same one the morgue technician had just left through.

"I'm sorry you had to go through that, sir. We were all certain it was her. We really thought it was Lillian. We found the body in the driver's seat of her car. The ID was there. The description matched. We're sorry you had to go through this but we're happy it's not your wife. Let's get out of here and then we'll talk about where we proceed from here. Let's go, sir."

The next round of silence ensued. Then they all left. Back through the same corridors under those God awful fluorescent lights. Past the security guy. Out the front doors. Back into the same car. The reverse drive back to his house, mostly in silence.

Although Gabriel continued to suffer through his shocking experiences of the night, there was a more essential and extreme sense of relief. It was not his Lillian who was on the morgue table tonight. That poor woman. Cold. Dead. Lifeless. Battered beyond belief. After what he'd gone through tonight, Gabriel prayed that the family she belonged to would be able to deal with her death and all that had led up to it. That they would have some relief and closure knowing that she was in heaven with God. That her suffering had ended. That God would help them through their own grief. Gabriel wondered if she had kids. A husband who missed her and loved her and wondered where she was. A family to grieve over her as she was buried and put to rest. Perhaps one day, when his own ordeal was over, he would find her cemetery plot and perhaps her family and express his condolences. That poor woman. That she was dead and that her monster torturer was still alive and breathing and out there and ready to do the same thing to someone else infuriated him.

As the drive continued so did Gabriel's reflections. He refocused his thoughts back to his own world. That wasn't her. It wasn't Lillian. So where was she? What was going on? Would she be at home in the kitchen when he got back and wondering where he had been? If he examined his own spidey-sense then he intrinsically knew his fantasy would not be true. He just knew it. Why was that poor battered woman wearing Lillian's dress? That beautiful red silk one that he knew so well. Why? And to add to things, why was that dead woman bathed in the same scent that his Lillian wore? What did that coincidence mean? Beyond that, how could that woman look so much like his Lillian? And why had she been in Lillian's car? In the driver's seat? And what kind of an incident had the car and its passenger been in? What weren't the other guys in the car telling him? And given that the dead body was not Lillian, who the heck was she? And again, where was the boy? So many questions rattled through Gabriel's brain over and over again, new questions and repeats of the same questions. His head started to ache. No reason it shouldn't match the rest of his body.

Gabriel's ruminations continued as he clutched the little piece of red silk from Lillian's dress (really her dress?). The drive continued and the men kept their silence. They must wonder as well, he thought to himself.

His head began to hurt even worse as all of these thoughts continued crashing in. He really needed to take some Advil as soon as he got home or he'd be in for an even larger world of hurt and truly unable to form a coherent thought. The rest of the car ride passed largely in an uncomfortable silence. The two men were not sure what they should be saying to him, so quiet was the best option.

They were a few miles from his house when one of the blokes spoke up. Silence broken.

"Gabriel, we need your help so we can help you. We're going to ask you questions once we get back to your house, like: Can you please tell us what Lillian's schedule was today? When did she leave home? Was her schedule predictable? Did she always drive the same route? And how did the boy fit into her itinerary? What pattern did she follow? When did you really feel she was missing? Who hated her? What can you tell us about why she is missing? Who would want to kill her or make it look like they killed her? What was she doing here? What was she doing with you?"

Gabriel sighed as the man's diatribe petered off and ended. He just looked out the car window as the miles passed. There was not much to see at this hour of darkness. It seemed the men had the same questions as he did, in addition to some new ones. Gabriel was totally and immensely disturbed. There was a very long pause and another heavy sigh before he answered. And he answered carefully and deliberately, beyond what he should even be capable of. But he knew silence was golden, that less was more, especially in these kinds of circumstances. The two men seemed to wait and hang on for his response.

"My Lillian left home at the usual time this morning."

Gabriel paused, then continued.

"She left with the boy, as she always did. Lillian always dropped him off on her way to work. Every day."

Gabriel choked out a sob before he regained himself as he went on.

"I love that boy as if he was my own. I can't even fathom where he is right now. Where his mother is right now. What has happened to them. I just don't know! Did he even go to school today? It was just a normal day when we all got started this morning."

Gabriel stared at the men in the front of the car, waiting for a suitable response.

The same man spoke. Again. "Sir. We need to file a report when we get you home. Plus for Lillian and the boy we need to file a missing person's report. Immediately. It's not over the 24-48 hour rule but we're going to prepare and file anyways because we have extenuating circumstances here. Her car. The unknown Jane Doe wearing Lillian's dress as well as her perfume. Clearly very badly beaten. Dead. With no sign of a child, a boy, anywhere."

He paused for a moment. Took a sip of his water bottle. Weighed what he had to say next. After all of these years on the job, these things never got any easier.

"Listen. I know this is hard for you. Very hard for you. We've seen many people struggle with this, but right now we need you to focus. Time is paramount. That woman back there is dead. Any thoughts and information you might have about her are valuable to us. Beyond that we need a profile from you about your Lillian. We need that to be able to start our investigation and do our best to bring her, and the boy, back to you as soon as possible so your life can continue, move forward. We need to try to find them and bring them back to you as soon as possible. Please help us. Please gather your thoughts so we can get as much information as possible as soon as we're back at your house. Now, please, just think through the first set of questions as best as you can."

The man paused again. Waited for Gabriel's reply.

Waited a little longer.

Gabriel sighed heavily again. He chewed through is answer before responding.

"I will do anything and everything I need to do in order to bring my Lillian home, bring the boy home, bring my family back together and back home. It may be a little family and it may be inconsequential to all of you but it's mine. It was mine. It still is mine and I want it back. As soon as possible. So just tell me what you need to know."

His eyes continued to fixate on the continuing landscape. As the roadside passed he felt an impending and increasing sense of desolation and loneliness. An emptiness as the car pulled into his own driveway. He got out of the car and stumbled to the house. He longed for a good long stiff drink before this nightmare continued. He headed through the front door, that big wooden one that he and Lillian had selected. He walked right into the kitchen. There was a bottle in the cupboard, the stiff stuff. That's what he needed right at this moment to stabilize himself and get on with what he needed to get on with.

The other men followed Gabriel in his silence. Theirs continued as well. He didn't bother to offer them any coffee or libation. They watched him as he walked over and poured himself four fingers of Sterling. Watched as he guzzled at least half of it in the first gulp. It was an almost absent reach down when he bent over and stroked Humphrey's fur. An afterthought. The dog enjoyed having his ears and neck stroked. The men just watched as the dog sat quietly by Gabriel's side.

In some weird way, the dog seemed to sense Gabriel's intense distress and just absorbed it. He cowered a little when Gabriel spoke to him.

"It's a fucked up day for sure. Where is our Lillian? We know she's not on the morgue table. Where is our boy? Can you reach out to the school and find out if my son was absent today? They didn't call me. What in the world happened to them? What's with the car too?"

He looked into those deep brown doggy eyes and didn't get an answer there either.

Then he looked over at the men. They looked very uncomfortable in their bedraggled suits. He was sure this was nothing new for them. He felt a little inhospitable at this particular moment.

"Is there anything I can get you guys? I'm not used to this kind of thing. I needed a stiff belt after what I've seen and been through in the last few hours. My life is totally upside down. The bottle's here. The glasses are in the cupboard. Help yourselves if you want some." With that, he topped off his own glass and walked over to the kitchen table. Humphrey still at his side. He sat down heavily and took another long sip. "I'm ready when you are."

The men just shook their heads at the offer of a drink and then one of the guys piped up and offered to make some coffee. His voice was surreal to Gabriel as he spoke. "Why don't I make a pot of coffee for all of us? We have questions. We understand you're upset. And we need to work together to get to the bottom of what you're going through as well as what that other family who belongs to that woman is and will be going through. Let's try to find some answers. But let's start with a pot of coffee if that's okay. What do you think, Gabriel?"

Gabriel nodded his head silently. Let them drink his coffee. Him, he was going to keep drinking until some reasonable set of numbness set in.

The man went to the counter. The coffee maker was in the obvious place. Freshly ground espresso coffee was on the bottom shelf of the refrigerator. Understandably. He rifled through the cupboards to find the cups and saucers, then the little spoons, then the sugar. He put the alcohol back in the cupboard because he figured Gabriel didn't need any more liquor than he'd consumed already in the last few minutes, although both he and his colleague could surely use a hit at this point in their day. Several as a matter of fact.

Gabriel spoke once more and rose from his seat. "Gentlemen. I need a few moments here. I'm going to go find my cat Bogart. Please excuse me for a bit. Humphrey, my boy, come with me. Let's find your feline friend. Do you know where he is?" Humphrey just looked at his master and whined a little. Odd, thought Gabriel. The dog wasn't normally a whiner.

With those words, Gabriel walked out of the kitchen in search of his cat. The man and his dog prowled through the house, opening doors, calling out for Bogart, turning lights on and then off. After a few extended minutes, Gabriel's calls for Bogart became a little louder and seemed to be more urgent. The men in the kitchen heard him offer a treat of canned tuna as incentive to come out from his hiding place. Bogart loved tuna. Nothing, no mice or birds or anything else got that cat going more than a can of fish. But where was he?

Gabriel walked into their bedroom and stopped dead in his tracks after he turned on the lights. Humphrey was right by his side. The hair just stood up on the back of his neck. He'd never really understood that expression until now, when he actually felt it. He was sure the dog felt it too as he growled low in his throat. Gabriel's mind rushed through thoughts at light speed. How was this even possible?

There, hanging from the closet door was a red dress. Lillian's red dress. It hadn't been there earlier before he went out. How was it there now? How did it get there? What the hell was going on?

His stomach rolled and turned. His heart felt like it was going to pop right out of his chest. Beads of sweat formed on his forehead and started to run down his face. His mind couldn't make sense of what was in front of his eyes. It was all so surreal for him.

Then his phone rang. He looked down at the display after he had pulled it from his pocket. Unknown caller. His belly roiled as he answered. He was ready to be sick.

"Hello."

There was a chuckle on the other end after he answered. His blood got colder than it already was. He wasn't ready for this at all.

"You're going to get to know me very well. And you're going to understand just how methodical and patient I am. Just you wait. You and I are going to have such a lovely relationship. Plus, please tell me how much you appreciated the work I did on the woman in the morgue. I took my time. Enjoyed it all fiercely. She didn't have such a great time. But at least I did. How did you like it? Did you pick up on all of the special touches? She was very unhappy with all of those details. But it was all for me and you, not for her."

Another sick and disturbing chuckle.

"My dear fellow. Take a deep breath. And, while I have you on the phone, and I need to go soon so this call cannot be traced, please do me a favour and stop looking for Bogart. You're not going to find him. He's not there. He was around when I brought the dress in, wasn't that a nice touch by the way? But he's not there now. Enjoy your night. Enjoy your dog. And have a wonderful night my friend. Sweet dreams. Oh, and before I forget, lose those cops that picked you up. The more you talk to them, the harder things will go for your pretty lady. Remember, I'll know what you do."

The connection ended abruptly, as much as it had started. The click was audible. Humphrey kept his gaze on Gabriel, watching and waiting in his doggy way. He startled as he heard his owner's cry, something bare and naked from deep within. Almost ancient.

Gabriel felt light headed as he put the phone back in his pocket and just surveyed the bedroom. His eyes settled once more on the red dress hanging from the door. How could her dress be there? He walked over towards it, his dog by his side. He could smell Lillian's perfume, her signature scent yet again, as he got closer to the closet and the dress. He was flabbergasted as he noticed there was a piece missing from the bottom hem. Identical to the piece he had in his pocket from the morgue. How? What? Why? This was impossible, yet here he was and there it was. And now he knew his spidey sense was for real, on track in some sort of weird way. His Lillian wasn't here. The boy wasn't here. And he knew now for a fact that his cat Bogart wasn't here at home either. Everyone was gone, except for those guys downstairs and that strange man on the phone and his canine by his side. He heaved a very heavy sigh as he collected himself and started that walk downstairs to deal with those men in his kitchen. He prayed to God that whatever he said to them would not in any way make things worse for Lillian. Or the boy. Or his cat. How did the guy on the phone know anything about his whereabouts and what he did and said? Were there hidden cameras or microphones in his house? How in the world did his life turn so upside down in less than a day? Gabriel felt hollow. At this point he was just a man and his dog, headed to the kitchen to deal with a pair of strangers. People who might be able to help him, but still people he needed to get rid of as quickly as possible. What to do? He felt lost and alone, desperate too. He did the best he could at this moment. He was a man after all. He sucked it up, swallowed his fear and misery, and walked into his kitchen to deal with them. His dog was by his side as he addressed the men in front of him.

"Now what?"

Humphrey glared at them simultaneously with his master. His doggy heart also beat through his chest, just like Gabriel's. The smell of freshly ground and brewed coffee hung thickly in the air. The cups and all of the accoutrements were present on the table.

The men were a little taken back by Gabriel's approach, but managed to keep it together fast.

The one man asked, "Did you find your cat, sir?"

"No. He's not here."

"Why not? Did you let him out earlier?"

"No. He's an indoor cat. He only goes out with us in the car or on a leash. He is pretty content just eating, going in his litter box, and then moving around the house to find the warmest sunniest spot he can to just lie down and have a nap, a cat nap. He's not here. He would've come to me when I called for him if he was here."

"So where do you think your cat is if he's not here?"

Humphrey gave a little doggy whine as Gabriel answered.

"I believe he's with Lillian. And probably the boy too. So where are they all? And, to repeat my question, Now What? What do we do now?"

The men just looked at him and the guy who spoke said, "Let's start with a cup of coffee. Let's start at the beginning. Please sit with us so we can help you as you help us. We're as lost as you are. Let's move this forward together. As a team."

"Okay."

He sat back down in his chair at the kitchen table and breathed in the steam from his cup of coffee. Humphrey sat by his side and waited patiently. No table scraps in sight today, but he knew he was needed and stayed sitting upright in his place.

TWENTY SEVEN

SEVEN YEARS AGO

Lillian breezed confidently into Gabriel's office after Mrs. Johnstock reluctantly showed her in. The sunlight coming through his windows shone on her hair, making it look more angelic than just blonde. For some reason her eyes seemed even bluer than he remembered. Her eyes and her skin appeared almost translucent. Gabriel's heart fluttered as he recalled their encounter a few days ago. This woman was having a huge impact on him. This was not something he was used to in his world. He was a goner.

Lillian walked up to his desk and stuck her hand out. She was confident. He wasn't sure if he could get up, or, if he was honest, not even sure he should stand up (if you know what I mean). So he stood part way. Most of what needed to be concealed, was. He took her hand and shook it. It was cool, dry and smooth. She had lovely long fingers, he noticed. And a firm handshake. Lillian looked directly at him as she spoke.

"It's so nice to see you again Gabriel."

There was a twinkle in her eyes as she spoke to him and it made him even more nervous and melted his heart further. There was another one of those pregnant pauses that writers always put into their stories, but this one was real as she spoke again, after Gabriel failed to release her hand.

"I hope you haven't changed your mind. If you would please let go of my hand, perhaps I can sit down and we could talk further?"

She laughed out loud. He acquiesced and let go. He was stunned because it was the first time he'd actually heard her laugh. Before he knew it, Lillian sat down and crossed her lovely legs in front of him without his invitation. He felt like a bit of a dufuss as he unceremoniously sat down behind his own desk and advised her, "I haven't changed my mind. When I give my word, I stay true to it. Now, let's get started on what you need."

Lillian looked at him so seriously, a little taken back with his direct reply. Those beautiful eyes of hers became guarded. Then she answered gently. "I need what I told you the other night. I need for us to both stop running, my son and I. I could run for my entire life if I needed to, but my little boy can't anymore. He needs to stop. He needs a life. He needs a home. He needs to be settled and stable. I need for him to go to a school with other decent kids his own age and make friends. He shouldn't be home-schooled for his entire childhood life. And he shouldn't spend most of his time sleeping in barely decent hotel or motel rooms scraping by with his mother." Lillian took a long pause at that point before continuing. She was assessing Gabriel as he sat in his chair behind his desk, while he listened to her diatribe.

"The first thing he really needs is a new name and to be officially enrolled in a decent school with a reputable address. Then I'm hoping he can learn properly with the other children and get socialized with his own peer group. That would be the best place for him to start."

Gabriel sat back in his chair and laced his hands behind his head again. He seriously regarded this lovely woman seated in front of him. He felt himself falling in love with her. Strange. Never in his life had he felt this way. She was unique and interesting to him. Confident. Yet compassionate. He thought of the best description for her. It was the name of a song he had often enjoyed. "The Untouchable One". That was her. It named her to precision. He let out a sigh and then spoke.

"What name do you want for your boy?"

Lillian was clearly taken back by his forthrightness and similarly sat back in her own chair before she spoke. Her eyes held his.

"I always liked the name Stewart. It always brought me back to all of those old romantic movies." Her face shone with a sense of a better time, she was nostalgic in her own way. He brought her out of her reverie with his next question, and not in a bad way.

"What surname would you like for him Lillian? As we do this, how do we do this right?"

Gabriel continued to sit back. Patient. Waiting for her.

She paused for a while before she spoke.

"I don't think he should have the same surname as me from here on in, just in case we get located again. Would you have any ideas please? Just something that makes sense for him."

Gabriel thought about all of this as he sat there. He thought about the boy. He thought about the woman in front of him. He thought about everything they'd said over their last few exchanges. And, simply, he just sat there and thought. Then he answered, with a small smile on his face, "If you really like all of the old films, why not switch up the names and make the boy Stewart James. Not James Stewart, but Stewart James. What do you think?"

It took Lillian quite a few moments to digest his suggestion and really make the connection. Gabriel could have lit up an entire rainbow when he saw her pretty face light up with a smile beyond anything you he could have imagined. It was glorious.

"I love it! James Stewart in reverse! You are so brilliant! Now, let's get to the details. What kind of paperwork do we need to get done, how do we do it? How can you help me wade through it? All of it? Please? Please help us."

With that outburst Lillian sat back in her own chair and paused. Her pretty legs were still crossed as she looked at him. As they regarded each other, Gabriel saw Lillian's sincerity and the hopefulness in her face. And her posture and mostly also in her eyes. That gaze broke into him somehow. It all touched him. Affected him. Disturbed him.

After their semi-companionable silence, Gabriel finally spoke and answered Lillian. "Yes, Lillian. I will help you. We will get through all of this together. I have faith that everything will work out just fine. Why don't you come by the house tonight? Google and print out all of the name change documents you need and bring along all of that paperwork and we'll figure it out over dinner? Plus, it does strike me that you and your son should have the same surname. Otherwise it will raise eyebrows. So print out paperwork for yourself."

Lillian contemplated him from her seat across the desk. She was clearly wary but needed someone to trust. She was banking on him to be that man. It wasn't like her to look for someone to help her. She never looked for a rescuer or a saviour. She was a strong and tough woman that relied on herself. But at this point she was starting to break down. It wasn't just her anymore. It also mattered to her little boy, and the way they were living was starting to affect him. Life on the lamb just wasn't something suited for a little boy. But he was hers and she loved him and wanted to do the very best for him so he could have a great life.

"I don't usually go to strange men's houses. And I have my son to contend with. He's not old enough to be allowed to be left on his own for the evening. Are you okay if I bring Mr. Stewart James along? I'm sure he'll like you a lot, I'm sure he's going to love his new name, and I really think the two of you would get along famously. Would that really be okay?"

It was clear to Gabriel that Lillian really didn't trust anyone. She was not just man-shy but really more so people-shy. He understood how much she was sending him an olive branch during their conversation. This was really difficult for her.

Gabriel gave her a very gentle smile and then told her it would all be okay. That he looked forward to meeting her son. Mr. Stewart

James. His smile said it all. "I'll be so happy to meet the mini-version of James Stewart!"

Both Lillian and Gabriel shared a laugh in their respective chairs. The sunlight continued to stream into his office as they both sat there and enjoyed the moment. Gabriel was slightly afraid that Mrs. Johnstock was going to break in at any moment and interrupt them. But ultimately she did not.

Lillian broke the moment by asking, "What time should we both be there tonight? What's good for you? And what should we bring?"

The glow on Gabriel's face was clearly visible. And he flushed more than a little bit as his heart rate increased during this exchange.

"Why don't you both come by around 5:30 or 6? There will be enough time and light left that Stewart can play with Humphrey a little bit. We'll see who wears whom out first. At the same time you and I can walk through whatever paperwork is going to be needed in relative privacy. Humphrey will be absolutely delighted to have a little boy around for once and I'm going to be thrilled to have more time in your company, selfishly."

His admission startled both of them. From his side he spoke from somewhere inside. His face got a little bit more flushed. She had not expected his words either and was taken aback, in a nice way, an unfamiliar way. He felt like he needed to bluster through a little bit so as to ensure he did not scare her off.

"We'll just throw some steaks on the BBQ and have a salad to go with it. I'll toss on a burger for young Stewart. Plus I have a very nice bottle of Merlot I've been saving for company, and I don't have company much, so it should be good and ready for tonight. We'll get the paperwork done, have a lovely evening, and still manage to get Stewart home for bed at a reasonable hour. Does all of that work okay for you?"

Lillian digested this man in front of her and replied very simply.

"We'll be there. But you need to tell me where to go and what we should bring."

"I'm just in a little place on the edge of town. Always had some dreams of someplace different. Just never found the right one. Humphrey and I are at number 23 Star Drive. There's no need to bring anything, I've got all the fixings there. Just bring young Mr. Stewart. And tell me know if he's allergic to anything. Like dogs or meat or milk." Gabriel chuckled as he added that last little bit in and hoped that his humour landed okay with her.

It seemed like it did. "He's fine with dogs and dirt and anything that gets put onto his plate to give him that next burst of energy."

The next silent pause seemed a little bit more companionable. Then she spoke again as she rose up out of her chair. Those long legs and beautiful body with that pretty face just mesmerized Gabriel. She stuck her hand out and said, "Thank you for your kindness. I have to go now. Be ready for us to bring a surprise for dinner, we never come without a little something. We'll be there. And I look forward to it Gabriel." Her hand was small and warm and dry in his. His hand was a little clammy from his nervousness.

"Humphrey and I will see you then."

With that, Lillian walked out of his office and he felt again like the room was terribly more empty than it had ever been. He sighed and sat back in his chair, trying to absorb what was now happening in his life. Wondering to himself what was going to happen with this lovely woman who had somehow captured his interest. It just wasn't like him. What was the good Lord bringing to his table now? He felt like he should hang on for the ride.

It wasn't long before Mrs. Johnstock burst in with the next thing he needed to get done.

TWENTY EIGHT
CURRENT NIGHT

Gabriel and Bogart may as well have been glued together as they huddled on the cheap worn-out bed of that sleazy motel room. Thoughts ran through Gabriel's head like a freight train out of control. He sobbed quietly into Bogart's soft fur. He could still smell Lillian's scent there. How was any of this even possible? Was it really Lillian on the other end of the phone or was this guy just messing with his head and playing a recording? Gabriel's heart and chest constricted as he cried out in a soulful longing for his Lillian, for his wife. His beautiful wife. He was a man just tapped out totally. His crying had contained jaunts of body convulsions that simply left him drained. The unanswered questions continued to run through his head. He felt lost and soulless. His contemplations were broken by a soft tap on the doorframe of the adjoining room. It was Liam. He was quiet and reserved as he brought in the kitty litter, a couple of little bowls, and a few bottles of water. The cat food followed.

"Hey dude, I don't trust the tap water in this dive for us, so I'm not taking a chance with Mr. Furry there either. None of us needs to know what happens to a cat when he gets Montezuma's revenge. So please do me a favour now that I've collected everything from that fat excuse for a woman downstairs and get your ass out of bed, and then get that cat organized and fed. Who knows how long it's been since he's had any kitty cat libations or a bio-break. I'm going to be just over here next door to try to dig for some more information and answers. Get up, my friend and pull your load. It'll help keep your mind clearer."

Gabriel nodded as he stood, still not letting go of Bogart, still reeling from the shock of what continued to transpire in his life.

"Joe and Frank are out scrounging for some decent take-out, if that's even possible in this dump of a country, as well as a case of beer. Hot food and cold beer...good luck with that here. It's been a long couple of days for both of us my friend as well as our team and we all need to eat and just chill for a bit. Go on and get going with Bogart. I'll call you when it's chow time or when I have some more answers." With that he patted Gabriel on his back and smiled kindly at him. Then Liam turned around and walked away. He strode through his adjoining door purposefully. He had calls to make and a whole pile of research to do. Liam expected Gabriel to keep it together for now at least, especially with Bogart there.

Gabriel watched Liam leave and saw the definitive ramrod defiance in his stiff back although the weariness was apparent. His own back bore the signs of disappointment and dejectedness with the anticipation of more waiting. He sighed heavily and clutched Bogart even closer. The feline squirmed with discomfort on that squeeze, but he stayed tight. The purring lessened a little bit, but still continued. Gabriel shoved himself off of the bed.

"Let's go Bogart. Let's get you organized in this dump my little buddy. Some food. Some water, but not tap water. And your own personal cat bathroom. Maybe by the time we get you sorted out then there might be some sustenance or relief for me. After all, we are in paradise, right my little friend?" Gabriel chuckled a little offhandedly in a distracted fashion and started to get Bogart organized.

Liam heard Gabriel's ministrations from the adjoining room and thought his comrade would be okay for now, at least with something productive to do. But it was time for him to focus. He needed to concentrate on what was going on, what the hell had brought them here, and what in the world could possibly be going on. Not to mention their next steps. Many times on these missions, especially the ones that took a long time, as their ringleader, Liam felt like the weight of the world was on his shoulders to carry. Some days he thought about Jesus and felt aligned with Him in His passion. His own sigh was heavy as he turned on his laptop and started to dig in the dingy light at the rickety table with the highly uncomfortable chair under his butt.

He wondered what in creation this night would bring to them, what was in store, would they be ready, would they survive it? Physically? Mentally? Emotionally?

His gaze travelled to his login display on the screen and he went to work. He had a job to do, after all. More than ever, he needed to get it done now. His fingers started on the keyboard almost of their own accord.

TWENTY NINE

THREE YEARS AGO

Gabriel looked at the two strange men, strange to him anyways. They were all still sitting in the kitchen. A cup of coffee in front of each of them. Steaming. Black. Hot.

Gabriel spoke again. "Now what?"

The two numb nuts, which is what Gabriel thought of them at this point, looked at each other in silence. Speech is golden. Silence is Silver. So Gabriel dug into his rage deeply and roared at the two men unexpectedly. "You guys are totally useless! How the fuck do you come into my home...my HOME!...and tell me there's been an accident and you're here to drive me to the fucking morgue to identify my wife? A woman who has clearly been butchered and beaten beyond belief! You make me suffer through your arrival. Your bungled little speech to get me into your car. The horrendous trip to the morgue. The process to get in there and deal with the little fucking details. And then. AND THEN. You show me the body. Well, the remnants of the body left behind. I suffer as I see her blonde hair. Her red silk dress. The way she had been mutilated. And then. AND THEN! When I get her turned over, I see for a fact that it is NOT MY FUCKING WIFE! How do you possibly, in the entire world, do this to a sane and peace loving husband and human being? How do you now stand there in my fucking kitchen like a pair of useless assholes, which by the way you are, while my existing, so far not-dead, wife is still alive and missing? And the boy is gone! He's never hurt a fucking fly in his life and he needs to count on you two to rescue him? Well, he would have been better hanging himself or trying to slit his wrists in the bathtub than wait for you guys to save him! Now where is my wife? Where is the boy? What are you two idiots doing to fix this situation? And, oh, please let me not forget, but maybe the SPCA would be more help than you guys, this guy also has MY FUCKING CAT! The same guy who butchered that poor woman on the slab at the morgue. He has my wife and my boy and my cat. And MY PATIENCE! If you have any humanity at all, the two of you will make damn sure that the next guy you launch yourselves onto is actually the husband of the dead woman, because you do not want to do this to another human being, ever. Now, in my most calm and rational voice I'm asking the two of you, WHY ARE YOU SITTING THERE LOOKING AT EACH OTHER? Get the fuck out of my house and hunt down this monster. He has no place on this planet. Bring my beautiful wife back to me. Bring the boy back. And, unless the SPCA does it first, bring back my fucking cat!"

By the time he was finished with his diatribe, Gabriel was flushed, sweating, and panting. The men could tell he was greatly agitated. They shuffled their feet on the floor underneath their chairs. Eye contact was pretty much non-existent. The pause in conversation was lengthy under these conditions. The fridge hummed in the background. Eventually, the one guy spoke up. "Listen, sir, we're very sorry for your trouble and the stress this whole situation plus the trip to the morgue has caused you. We would like you to understand that we fully believed it was her. Lillian. Your wife. It looked like her from the DMV photo. Plus her purse was there. We were anxious to notify and resolve a very horrible situation as quickly as possible so we could hunt down the killer. The murderer. In doing so we've managed to dislodge you emotionally and we're sorry for that. Very sorry."

Another pause transpired after the man spoke. Gabriel remained staunch and silent. The other, non-speaking guy, continued to avoid speaking. Then, after a bit, the man spoke again. Deliberately, this time. And much more slowly. " We were clearly wrong in everything, sir. Our approach. Our haste to find resolution for a dead woman whom we thought was your wife based on the information at hand. And now we face two situations that we will work on. That dead butchered woman in the morgue has a family somewhere. We don't know if she has a husband, children, parents, or other family. But we need to do our jobs to bring her home. We also now have a live case to pursue the monster who did what he did to her. It may be the same monster as yours. It could be a team working together to accomplish such a nightmare. The additional situation we are now engaged in is yours. It matters to us more than the other situation in terms of the fact that your wife and the boy are still alive from what we understand now. I'm asking you to step up and work with me. To start from the beginning and then let's see what kind of progress we can make from here. Together. As quickly as possible."

Another silent pause ensued. Gabriel looked into the man's eyes and waited. The other man sighed very heavily as he extended his hand toward Gabriel and replaced his steely gaze with a new kind of kindness in his eyes before he said, "Gabriel, my name is Liam and I want to help you."

Gabriel regained his earlier calmness and took his hand, somewhat reluctantly, still with trepidation. It was warm to the touch. Dry. Firm. But somehow gentle and sympathetic. This guy must have done many of these calls in his career and was by now very good at it. As Gabriel assessed Liam's eyes he clearly saw many years and many events of human pain and tragedy. Somehow, in some strange way, Gabriel felt like he could trust this man. With his free hand he absently stroked Humphrey's soft fur at the top of his doggy skull before answering. "Okay. Let's sit down together and see what we can get figured out. BUT, if at any point in time I think you're not being honest with me or I think you're not disclosing something, I will nail you to the cross and tell you to get the fuck out of my way. At which point I will do this alone. If we have a deal then let's sit down and get started before I change my mind."

Liam nodded in acknowledgement and the three men settled in more comfortably at the kitchen table. They each took a pull from their coffee and Gabriel took an extra sip from his drink to boot. No other sustenance was offered to the men by Gabriel. They just had the stark and empty table between them, going hand in hand with the empty silence. Moments went by and then Liam cleared his throat and spoke as he pulled out his notepad. "Gabriel, I know how hard this is for you. Trust me I know and one day I'll tell you my story. But for now, please, let's start with today and what you remember about the day. Was it a normal day or did anything different happen? The devil's in the details as you know, so I need you to recount anything and everything that was a departure from the usual routine you guys had. Please don't leave anything out."

Gabriel's anger and aggression returned and he choked on his next words as he spat them out. "I suppose you want to know if I fucked my beautiful wife this morning before we left our bedroom. Did I slap her ass? Did I make her suck my cock? Did I pull her hair? Make her watch something on our big screen TV? Shall I start there or can you understand that I am a man who is lost without his beautiful wife, who would never do anything to hurt her. We have a great relationship together, we're lovers and best friends. We talk and we cook and we make love and we get wild, together and consensually. So where do you want me to start, Liam?"

Liam held Gabriel's gaze steadily. He understood the man's frustrations. And he knew the sincerity that was there and that now was the time to cut him some slack. This was not a man who raped and mutilated and murdered his wife. This was a man who was distraught and in anguish and wanting to know where his wife and family was right now. "Please understand you are not under investigation here. You're part of our team right now and the most important aspect is to find your wife, your family. I don't need any bedroom details my friend, just please tell us about the rest of the day as best you can."

Gabriel only hesitated briefly before answering. "Today was normal by most accounts. We all had breakfast together before she left with the boy. Egg whites for her fried up with some hot peppers and ketchup. Lord only knows how she eats that, but it's what she likes. Cereal for the boy. And bacon mixed with the leftover egg yolks on toast for me. Lord knows that woman taught me never to waste a single morsel of food. We had our coffees and the boy had his milk. I washed the dishes, she dried them and the boy put them away. Just like we do every day. Then she got him sorted out to head to school and kissed me goodbye before she left. Lillian always took the boy to school." Gabriel's eyes raised up to the men with his next question, "Have you even checked with the school this afternoon? Did the boy make it there today? I didn't get a call that he was absent. Was he there? Where is he?"

Liam sat even further back in his chair now. His gaze travelled over to his colleague. "Go make the calls you need to make Joe. You, of all people, know exactly what we need to do now and how time is of the essence. Please make your calls from another room, as fast as you can. Get whomever out of bed you need to. If anyone complains tell them to call me or fire me. I'll bear the brunt of it, as usual."

Joe. At least now Gabriel knew the other guy's name. Joe heaved his sturdy frame out of the kitchen chair. He announced he'd be making his calls from outside while he grabbed his requisite amount of "fresh air". For a solid man he moved quickly, with confidence, and with purpose. His footsteps echoed across the kitchen floor as he made his way to the back door. Gabriel and Liam watched him go in silence. Humphrey was even more watchful and alert than usual. His body gave away that he was tense. He stayed by Gabriel's side, closely. Gabriel continued to stroke Humphrey's soft head in an absent and distracted fashion.

The kitchen clock ticked painfully loudly in the silence that ensued, outdone only by the large grandfather clock in the hallway.

Liam leaned in to Gabriel as he finally spoke again. His words were sincere and to the point. "Listen, I understand your distress Gabriel. More than you know, I understand. But right now I need you to dig very deep and tell me everything you know about your wife Lillian and her past. If there's nothing that strikes you different about today then we need to go back. We need to understand everything that you know. The far away past and the recent past. Has anything changed recently, even if not today? What clues can you give us? What intel do you have in your brain that you can give to us so that we can explore what the hell is going on? We need to know where to start. Where to look. Where did you two meet? How did you meet? When? There are so many questions and I cannot help you unless you help me. Help us. You must know something." With that, Liam paused and waited. Silence always created an opportunity to allow a person to speak if they felt compelled to say something. Their breathing filled the room. The silence continued to be stifling. Liam waited. And waited. And then his patience paid off. Gabriel spoke. His voice was rife with emotion. Hoarse with the emotions the day had caused. Liam knew from instinct that this was not a man who had caused any harm to his family. He clearly missed and longed for his wife. Gabriel's words chilled Liam and gave him pause. After a long few minutes Gabriel's gaze wandered around the room and he swallowed hard, then focused back on Liam.

"I'll tell you everything I know. But you have to promise me that you will tell me everything you find along the way. Good or bad. Everything. And right away. Do we have a deal?"

Liam eyed Gabriel evenly and assessed him before he spoke. He sighed. Weighed his options. "Gabriel, we have a deal. Let's get started now. Right away. We need to find your wife, your family. As soon as humanly possible. Tell me what you know. Now, please."

Gabriel surprised Liam by leaning over to him and whispering in his ear. "Before I start, you have to know something. The monster was here in this house while we were out to the crash site and the morgue. He knows you're here now and he says he can listen to what we discuss and that if I say anything he'll hurt Lillian even more than he'd planned. Write me a note and tell me where and when to meet you after you leave. While we're here, let's not aggravate him. Please work with me. This is my love, my wife, my life, my family at stake."

Liam's expression went well past surprised as he digested this new information. But the man was a consummate professional. He regained his poise and nodded purposefully, yet discreetly. Good, thought Gabriel, they had an understanding.

Gabriel pretended to hang his head and then started to tell the story of his Lillian. One that would not tip off the monster, wherever he was and however he was listening. Liam knew the synopsis was vanilla-coated. Part way through Gabriel's story, he slipped him a card with a time and location on it where they could meet and speak freely without any risk to Lillian. Gabriel acknowledged the card when it hit his thigh and stuffed it into his pocket without even looking at it.

THIRTY

SEVEN YEARS AGO

Gabriel paced frantically between the kitchen and the front window. He was full of anticipation for Lillian and her son to arrive at his home. The house was reasonably clean. Given the time, the lights were on in the core of the house. As with all beloved animals who knew their families, Humphrey knew something was up and eyed Gabriel warily from his comfortable doggy bed in the corner of the homey kitchen. Even though the dog knew something was amiss, he still had that silly doggy look on his face he had had ever since Gabriel had arrived home with grocery bags full of food. Not the usual fare of take-out food. No pizza boxes. No frozen TV dinners. Real food. Fresh food. Humphrey could smell the fresh actual meat in one of the bags. His little doggy mind hoped he would be able to collect some table scraps once dinner was on the table. He kept his eyes on Gabriel as he moved around and worked on the food. Eagle eyes, for a dog at least.

Gabriel had a fresh salad already ready in the kitchen. Plus there was some garlic bread in the oven, pretty much ready to go. But the best part was in the assembly and creation of the homemade meatballs. Humphrey hoped for spillage as the meatballs were being created. He was rewarded for his prayers, at least a very little bit. Once made, the meatballs went into the beautiful smelling tomato sauce. Nothing smelled better than onions, garlic, mushrooms, parsley from the garden, oregano and home-made tomatoes simmering. Throw in those groovy meatballs and you had heaven on a plate. For most of his life, Gabriel had called his meatballs "Angel Meatballs". He had gotten his recipe started from his grandmother's recipe and had finally, after many years, perfected them. He complimented himself that they were pretty damned good. Just wait until they were paired with the sauce!

Gabriel eyed the table for the umpteenth time. Just like Humphrey eyed the stove and all the great smelling food his doggy nose could glean. The table had a clean tablecloth. Best dishes that Gabriel owned. At least they had no chips out of them. Or any worrisome cracks. The serviettes were out. Cutlery was in place. The red wine was decanted. Gabriel didn't know a lot about wine, but he did know enough to corral the dude at the liquor store and solicit his help. The guy was a lot younger than Gabriel, had a ponytail, but seemed to know what he was talking about. He seemed competent and confident as he directed Gabriel towards a bottle of Amarone. Gabriel nodded a lot. Thought the wine was a little on the pricey side, but bought two bottles just to make sure he had enough on hand. Made sure he understood the right way to open, wait, pour, etc. the stuff so he didn't look like a total bohemian. He also engaged the fellow to locate a good bottle of white wine, just in case Lillian didn't like red. Got a lesson on proper chilling and pouring for that one too. The guy sure knew his wine and how to serve it. For the most part, Gabriel just enjoyed his beer at the end of the day and then some not-so-occasional cognac with an occasional cigar. He'd decided to leave the ancient (huh) dusty bottle of Merlot where it was in the cantina. Someone had given it to him years ago and he didn't want to take a chance that maybe it had gone skunky. Better to be safe and buy something fresh for tonight.

So for now, the red wine was out and "breathing" as per the young wine dude at the store. And the white wine was in the fridge, clearly not "breathing" as per Mr. Ponytail. Guess that didn't need to have any fresh air with it. Everything was set. No candlelight. It wasn't like it would be a date with her son present. Gabriel had even gone out and bought milk and iced tea for the kid he'd never even met. He really had no idea what kids drank these days.

Gabriel sighed anxiously as he walked back to the front of the house yet again to see if he could see Lillian's car driving up his driveway. Humphrey tagged along constantly, probably wondering in his little doggy mind what the heck was going on today.

There was still no sign of her. Gabriel strolled back to the kitchen to check on the food. He expected she would be on-time and thus turned off the oven and stove, re-mixed his fresh salad and making sure, again, that the table was properly set. He picked out one of his grandmother's special bowls for the meatballs and a special platter for the garlic bread. He heard Humphrey whine a little as he turned back to the stove and started to load up the meatballs. That made Gabriel smile and take a little pity on the beast. He spared a meatball and chopped it up for the dog in his bowl. "Here you go boy. There will be more later if you're a good fella. Please mind your manners and don't beg at the table when they get here." The dog chowed down on the single meatball like it was his last dinner on earth. Gabriel smiled as he turned back to the stove to plate the food. The smells in the kitchen were making Gabriel's stomach growl worse than his dog's.

Then Gabriel heard the doorbell as he finished plating the food. Finally. But right on time. Gabriel's heart skipped a few beats as he walked to the front door. Humphrey had scarfed down his meatball and was now right by his side again. Gabriel sighed. There she was. Pretty as when she had come to his office, but somehow more beautiful tonight. With less make-up. Faded jeans that fit just right with rips in all the right places. Basic t-shirt that showed off her body. Clearly she worked out and stayed fit. Cool Keds on her bare feet. Gabriel could smell the light flowery scent of her perfume. But what tugged at Gabriel's heart was how gently yet protectively she had her arm around her quiet and handsome son. The boy clung to her as he stood a little bit back of her. Gabriel could sense trepidation, perhaps an underlayment of past fears haunting him. It was written all over the boy's face and showed in his body language, his posture. He looked vulnerable somehow, the eyes speaking of a place where early innocence had been shattered.

"Hello Lillian." Gabriel said as he shook her soft yet strong hand, gazing into her beautiful eyes for just one moment before releasing her hand and getting down on his haunches a bit. He stuck his hand out to the boy next and said, "You must be Stewart. I'm very pleased to meet you. I know I promised your mom steak for dinner but changed my mind and thought we'd have more of a guy meal tonight. I'll even give you a couple to sneak to my dog Humphrey, assuming he behaves like a gentleman. Then, after supper you can wear him out with the ball in the backyard. What do you think Stewart?"

The boy's handshake was tenuous and wary, but Gabriel could tell the ice was breaking as the corners of the boy's mouth turned up slightly. Gabriel wasn't sure if it was because of the meatballs or the dog or both. Regardless, the boy didn't speak.

Gabriel stood up, smiling gently, and caught a warm gaze from Lillian.

"Won't you come in please? Make yourselves comfortable over here at the table. Dinner is ready. I'm starving. I know Humphrey is out of his mind hungry, so I hope you two brought your appetite along too! Let's go eat."

With that, he led his guests down the hall to the dining room. Their footsteps echoed in the hall behind him and Humphrey's nails clicked along the floor next to him. Gabriel knew the dog hoped he'd be allowed into the dining room to share in the meal so he was nicely on his best doggy behavior. The table was set for just the three of them with Gabriel's place at the head, Lillian's on his right, and he'd thoughtfully placed Stewart's setting next to his mother's. Gabriel figured that would be more comfortable for the boy for this first meal together.

Lillian was delighted when she saw the setup. "Gabriel, this is lovely. Thank you so much. We would have been fine at the kitchen table too you know. But this is a very nice treat, isn't it Stewart?"

Stewart nodded and his shoulders loosened and dropped just slightly. Good, Gabriel thought, he's beginning to relax a little. As the two of them sat down, Humphrey did his part. The dog hedged his bets that the boy was the best opportunity for table snacks and planted himself expectantly at his side, tail wagging slowly, with his head resting on the boy's arm of his chair. Stewart put his hand on Humphrey's head and softly started to stroke it.

"OK, young man, what can I get you to drink? Water, ice tea, milk?" Gabriel asked. The boy looked up at his mother and got a slight nod before he said, "A soda would be lovely, sir." The boy's was very low, barely audible.

Gabriel smiled and said, "You've got it son as long as you promise not to call me sir again. It kind of makes me feel like I'm a senior citizen. And I still have a few years to go before I'm at that age. How about you call me Gabriel or Gabe for short? Depending on which one you pick I'll either call you Stewart or Stu. Do we have a deal?"

The boy was not used to being addressed in such a friendly relaxed fashion by a stranger and his voice remained low as he replied, "I'd like to call you Gabriel, sir." And then realized his faux pas, paused uneasily for a second or two until both Gabriel and Lillian broke out laughing, which caused him to smile quietly. The ice was slowly breaking.

"And for you, madam, what can I get you to drink? I have red wine that's been breathing for a little while and white wine that's been suffocating in the fridge all afternoon."

The smile stayed on Lillian's face as she spoke, "You must promise never to call me madam or any version thereof. I may be a little worn around the edges but I'm nowhere near being a senior citizen. You may be a lot closer than I am, but I'm going to hang onto my youth for as long as I possibly can! I'd say with meatballs, a glass of red wine would be wonderful, thank you sir." At that address, Gabriel rolled his eyes and Lillian laughed some more. Stewart's smile broadened a little further. Meanwhile Gabriel's heart melted even more.

"Coming right up!" With that he turned on his heels and strode into the kitchen.

Lillian called out after him, "Is there anything we can do to help?"

"No, thank you. It's all done. Just give me a sec to get the drinks and then I'll plate the food and we can chow down."

Gabriel was back quickly with the beverages and returned to the kitchen to load up the food platters, one for pasta, one for the meatballs and sauce, and one for the garlic bread. It all smelled wonderful. Gabriel smiled to himself as he imagined Humphrey's stomach growling in anticipation. As he carried in the serving dishes he was pleased to see the anticipation on Lillian's and her son's faces and he knew he'd been right to change the menu from steaks to this. Who didn't like Italian food?

Gabriel seated himself, placed his cloth napkin in his lap, and asked, "Do you mind if we have a short prayer together before we eat? I promise to make it short because I'm very hungry."

Lillian nodded her assent.

They all began with a sign of the cross and Gabriel started, "Lord, we thank You for this blessed day, for the wonderful guests I have sitting around my dining table, for Your hand in making sure I didn't botch my culinary adventure. Please bless us and grant us peace, friendship, and harmony. Now, if You don't mind, we're going to eat. Amen." Lillian and Stewart followed with their Amen's and they all made the sign of the cross again.

Lillian spoke first as Gabriel loaded up Stewart's plate before moving onto hers, "This looks and smells absolutely wonderful Gabriel. Thank you so much for inviting us over."

"You're welcome Lillian, it's my pleasure. Now Stewart, I've put a few sauce-less meatballs on an extra plate by your side. As long as Humphrey is a good boy, those are for him. Please let them cool off for a few minutes and then break them into smaller pieces and let him snack slowly. If we let him have them all on the plate at once, he'd have them eaten in about fifteen seconds and he'll be eyeballing your plate throughout the rest of the meal, which might be fun at first but tends to get bothersome after a while."

Gabriel settled down into his chair after loading up his plate and they all started to eat. He was pleased with the satisfying noises that came from Lillian and her boy. After the first few bites, Gabriel raised his glass and called for a toast, "To new friends and hopefully friendships that will last a very long time. Cheers!" They all clinked their glasses and sipped their beverages, then went right back to eating. Gabriel wondered how long it had been since they ate like this and even ate with an almost complete stranger. He was pleased to have them under his roof.

It wasn't long before their plates were clean. Once the meatballs had cooled a little Stewart had parcelled out small bites to Humphrey. The dog was in heaven between the boy and the meatballs. It seemed too that for this moment the boy was content and possibly partially happy. Lillian gave a heavy sigh as she complimented Gabriel, "That was absolutely fantastic. I was anticipating steak, but this was even better! Where on earth did you get that recipe? I have to admit I ate more than I should have and I'm so full. I'm ready for the couch, a pillow and a blanket. But I'll contain myself and help you clean up. Stewart, how did you like dinner?"

Stewart was still a little muffled as he answered, but a bit louder than before. "I loved it mom. I'd like to come back and eat here again, if that's okay."

Lillian and Gabriel laughed at the same time, with twinkles in their eyes. Lillian responded to her son, "Darling, anytime we are invited back here, I promise to bring you. Now, please be a good boy and carry all of our dishes over to the kitchen. I'll help Gabriel clean up. When you're done clearing the table, you can take the mutt outside in the backyard. We'll be able to see you from the kitchen the whole time. I want to see who wears whom out first. Now, way you go!"

Gabriel and Lillian sat quietly while Stewart cleared the table. Humphrey did not stray far from the boy's side. His new best friend. When Stewart was done he collected his shoes from the front door and led the dog out back. Humphrey knew it was time to play and raced to locate his ball, then brought it over to the boy. Stewart's laughter as they started to play was definitely infectious. In the meantime, Lillian and Gabriel went to work on the cleanup. She washed the dishes while Gabriel stored the leftovers, dried dishes along the way, and started on making some coffee. They worked companionably in silence, sipping the leftover wine in their glasses while also watching the boy with the dog.

Once the cleanup was done, Gabriel suggested to Lillian that they sit together at the kitchen table where they could watch Stewart as well as talk alone. Lillian let Gabriel know that she'd brought some apple pie for dessert. Gabriel let her know he had vanilla ice cream in the freezer for them so it was all a good match. "Let's have a little coffee and talk first. Let Stewart and Humphrey wear each other out and when they come in we'll break into dessert. Okay?"

Lillian simply nodded her agreement.

Gabriel started, open-ended, "Lillian, please, let's go through the paperwork you have and please fill in the blanks for me in terms of what's happened to you in your life. I'm not nosey or prying, I just want to get to know you and understand."

With that, Lillian smiled slightly and they got started. While they filled in documents, they talked and Stewart played outside gleefully with Humphrey. It was the happiest Lillian had seen her little boy in years.

THIRTY ONE
CURRENT NIGHT

Bogart stuck very close to Gabriel as his master organized the cat-fixings. Everything was very much appreciated by the feline even though this place in no way resembled a kitty-cat Hilton. First ready was the little litter box. Thank goodness because the cat clearly needed to use it. Bogart wrinkled his nose at the cat kibble. His disdain was malleable. The cat's reaction made Gabriel smile and chuckle a little, albeit sadly. The man just leaned against the filthy door jamb and watched his cat. Suddenly tears sprang into his eyes as he recalled the day he and Lillian and her little boy went shopping to go find a cat. They had figured a dog needed a cat to keep him in line, just like a man needed a woman for the same reason. They had trudged through shelters and pet stores and finally happened on a small, out of the way cat sanctuary. Bogart was a done deal for them from the moment the three of them laid eyes on him. Gabriel broke himself out of his reverie and pushed away from the doorway and back into his room. Back to this reality. A time and space with no reprieve or time for sentimentality. A place in time with no conclusion or answers for the man.

Gabriel sat down heavily on the sagging bed with its ancient covers that had seen Lord knows how many people in its time. The sound of Bogart crunching on his dry cat food broke through to him and was somehow comforting. He could also hear Liam in the adjacent room.

Typing for sure. And also on the phone with a very low, hushed voice. Gabriel had long since learned to never eavesdrop on any of Liam's calls or conversations and he wasn't about to trespass against that rule now. He knew unequivocally that Liam told him everything he learned about Lillian and her situation, past and present. He also knew that, sadly, Liam worked on a few of these kinds of dramas simultaneously at any given time. It was very sad that somehow this had become a new normal for them. Liam. Frank. Joe. Himself now too. Plus he knew about the others.

Bogart disturbed Gabriel's train of thought as he rubbed himself in and around and between his legs like only a cat can do. Guess he was done with his dinner. Now it was time for petting and purring followed closely by a cat nap.

"Come on boy." said Gabriel to the cat as he picked him up. "I wish you could tell me your secrets. Like where you have been. What you've seen. Who the Hell is doing this. And where my Lillian, my family, is right now so I could bring them home. Where are they? Oh, Bogart, how I wish you could talk now."

Gabriel buried his face yet again into Bogart's soft fur and began to cry again in his agony. He tried to be quiet so as not to alert they guys about how low he was really feeling right now. Gabriel was so lost that he didn't see Liam standing in the doorway. Probably more critically, he didn't hear what Liam was mumbling under his breath. "We have some of those answers my friend. But they all lead to other questions for which we don't have any answers at all. Yet. What a fucking journey this was and continues to be. I'll bet that if you wrote this whole experience into a book, no one would believe it. They'd think it was pure fiction."

Liam continued to stare at Gabriel for a long few moments. He reflected that, in these last few years, he had really come to like the man. Liam had found Gabriel to be very bristly when they had first met. But that was understandable. Any sort of decent bloke who cared about his family would be a tough customer in a situation like this. Over time, and the various predicaments they put themselves in (but let's be honest here for a moment. Predicaments they knowingly put themselves in.),

Liam could always count on Gabriel's empathy for the man they were trying to help. Gabriel trusted Liam to deliver the right instructions to the team and he did his part to execute on those explicitly even when things went FUBAR. Liam knew that Gabriel had an unwavering commitment to finding the truth and ultimately bringing the cases to conclusion, sometimes with very sad and disturbing answers. Liam figured it must weigh heavily on the man since he had years of almost no answers for himself at any juncture.

Liam sighed as he thought to himself, "Yes, Gabriel is a stand-up guy. A very unlikely recruit for sure, but he really brought value to the team. Gabriel never complained about spending time on someone else's situation even though his own was unresolved, and even at times at a stand-still. Sure, Gabriel was pushy, demanding and aggressive in his pursuit for answers. But what decent man wouldn't be? This was his family for crying out loud." Not only did Liam like Gabriel and trust him, but he definitely considered him a friend now. One born out of the most unlikely of circumstances. A solid friendship he appreciated nonetheless.

Liam's mental musings delivered another heavy sigh which was loud enough to cause Gabriel to pull his tear-addled face out of Bogart's fur as he turned slightly and faced Liam in the doorway. The expectant look on Gabriel's face caused even more anguish for Liam.

Before either man could speak, there was a knock on the door of Gabriel's room. The moment of silence and reverie was broken and shattered. Gabriel was quick to put Bogart into the bathroom in a near-total silence. He then moved towards the room door from the side, trying to keep safely out of the line of sight. In the meantime Liam had bolted into his room and picked up some weaponry. There wasn't an opportunity to call for Joe and Frank right now since they were out scrounging for grub.

Liam had his gun on the ready as he moved towards a shadowy corner of the room where he could see everything and mostly not be seen in the darkness and dinginess. He had clear line of sight on the door. It was almost magical how silently and fluidly both men moved, and with haste at the same time. But that came from the fact they'd done this together so many times before. In their downtime they joked a little about their "connection". Regardless, it worked for them. Call it their combined spidey-sense.

Gabriel and Liam made eye contact once they were in position and used their fingers to count down. Three. Two. One. Go! Gabriel yanked the motel room door open while Liam kept his gun trained on the person standing there. Both men were totally astonished to find a young boy, maybe ten years old, standing in front of them. Even more bizarre was that the child was holding a gift bag.

Gabriel was so stunned and shocked and speechless and motionless that Liam sprung into action. He started by pulling the boy into the room, a little roughly. Liam then scanned around the outside briefly, and, not seeing anyone or anything suspicious, he eased back into the room and secured the door.

Liam's face was set, firm, and all business as he turned to the little boy. "Who the fuck are you? Why are you here? Who fucking sent you? And what the fuck is in that bag?" Liam's voice was harsh and menacing. He made the boy tremble when he continued his tirade. "Speak! Now! Or I promise you won't live to see your next birthday!"

The boy trembled even more but wasn't nearly as shaken as he a normal boy would have been. This was a kid who had grown up on the streets in this Godforsaken place. He made no moves, barely breathed, and kept his eyes on Liam as well as the gun in Liam's hand.

"I am supposed to give this to you senior." Said the child as he indicated to and held out the gift bag. "I do not know what's in it Senior. Some man in the square paid me to bring it to this room." Then, as only a street urchin could and would do, he piped up with a little more courage, "The man told me Senior would tip me for this delivery." The boy visibly swallowed hard as he knew the lie he'd told about that, but he desperately wanted to eat well tonight and needed a little money in order to fill his empty tummy.

Liam's expression shifted ever so slightly and his demeanor cracked just a little too. This was clearly a runabout child. A small stranger who was used to life on the streets. A little boy struggling to survive on these harsh streets. He had to give the kid credit. He had balls, but dangerously so. And to ask for a tip to boot. It reminded Liam of men he'd known who had come from similar circumstances. Anything for an extra buck. And Liam knew that anything really did mean anything. As long as you weren't dead at the end of the night, maybe had some chow in your belly, maybe had some clothes on your back, and if you were really lucky had a safe place to sleep where no one would bother you. He often mused in the witching hours of the night why God delivered such suffering to children. He was certain he wasn't alone in asking that question. Grown-ups...well...just let them reap what they had sown. And old people, well he thought they should just be left in peace. Even through his ruminations Liam kept the gun pointed at the boy. After all, even though he was empathetic, he wasn't stupid. In this hell hole a small child could and would easily slit his throat for a few bucks or a piece.

Liam cleared his throat and spoke, "What's in the bag kid?"

The little boy just shrugged his shoulders as he replied back, "I have no idea Senior. The man in the square tell me to deliver the bag. He tell me not to look. If I look, he say he kill me. So I no look. And you Senior, you must pay me a good tip because I do good job for you." With that, the kid shuffled from one foot to another. Then back and forth. Uncomfortable. Out of his element and a little scared. But still balls to the wall in order to survive. His dark, almost black eyes stayed fixated on Liam. His breathing was a little fast. His little face was dirty and anxious. He was watching. Waiting.

Liam continued to fix his gaze upon the boy. Finally he spoke. "Who was the man? What did he look like?"

"I don't know Senior. It was just a man in the square. He came up behind me. Asked me not to turn around. Asked me if I wanted to make some money. I said yes, but I was afraid he was going to pull down my pants or make me turn around and do something for him, you know? But then he said he would pay me to deliver a bag. He told me the address, here. To this motel. Made me repeat it back to him so he knew that I understood where to go. He told me which room to come to. Then he put this bag in my one hand and put some money in my other hand. Then he kicked me in the ass and told me to get the job done right now. I never looked at him. I just ran all the way over here. And that's all I know Senior. Plus he tell me you give me a good tip for doing a good job." The kid swallowed even harder this time after he spoke.

After a long pause, Liam signalled Gabriel to take the bag from the kid. Gabriel did so after a few quick strides across the room. Liam shot the kid a hard long look and said, "If you didn't see him then at least tell me how he sounded. How he spoke to you. Did he speak English? Did he sound American? Or was he Spanish? A local?"

The kid swallowed hard again as he stuttered out his reply, "The voice belonged to a man like I told you. He spoke to me mostly in English and he sounded a lot like the American tourists we have around here. I don't know anything more than that Senior."

Liam sighed heavily and used his free hand to reach into his pants pocket to pull out some coins. As he handed them to the boy he said, "If this man finds you again then you need to get a good long look at him. I'm sure he's going to want to know his package got delivered and that you didn't just run off with it. If you come back and bring me any information about him like what he looks like and where he's staying then I will have more money for you. The more information you bring back, the more money there will be. I want to know who he is and where he's living. Bring your other friends into this if you need to follow him. I will pay for good information and the better the information the better I pay. But you never tell this man about our deal. You tell him you delivered the package, I waved a gun at you, didn't tip you and you ran off because I threatened to shoot you. Do you understand me little one? If you say anything to anyone about our deal, then I guarantee you I will find out and the deal is off. Now, take your money kid and get out of here. Run! Now!"

The boy grabbed the money in a flash and bolted the hell out of the room like only a street kid could. The door latched weakly. Liam reholstered his weapon and walked towards Gabriel saying, "Let's see about that bag my friend. But let's do so calmly and safely."

Both men walked over to the shitty table and chairs over by the window with its curtains (if you could call them that) drawn tightly. Gabriel put the bag down with a strange and uncomfortable look on his face. Somehow he sensed this would not be good. Bogart wove his little feline body in and out between his legs. Liam gently reached over to the bag and hefted it for weight. Then he peered at it extensively in the crap lighting of the room.

"I don't think we have a risk of explosives in here. For one, it's too light. Secondly, the guy in the square wanted this delivered and handing it to a kid if he had it loaded with explosives would have meant a possible non-delivery. Plus, whoever this guy is, I have a feeling he doesn't want to kill you, at least not with a sudden hit. I think he wants to hurt you mentally and emotionally. Kill you that way. Slowly. I think he's getting his rocks off by torturing you like this. He wants you to hurt badly. And, now we need to keep an eye out for him because he is going to want to see the damage he's done to you. Word of warning my friend, keep calm. No matter what happens, keep calm. Your team is here. I'm here. Now, let's open the bag my friend."

With a great deal of fear and anxiety, heart pumping, head pounding, hands shaking, Gabriel uttered a small prayer and then went forward with opening the bag handles with his clammy hands. After the handles were pried apart he pulled out the tissue paper. With Liam's eyes fixed upon him, Gabriel reached in and withdrew the contents. He gasped and tried to catch his breath as he saw what it was. A light blue colored baby rattle. With a note attached to it. His eyesight dimmed. His world went black. Liam tried but failed to catch his friend as Gabriel collapsed on the floor and passed out.

Liam thought to himself, "Man, Gabriel does that a lot."

THIRTY TWO

THREE YEARS AGO

After Gabriel spun a basic story about Lillian for Liam and then told him to get on his way with his buddy Joe, Gabriel looked at the card Liam had passed him. It said the men would meet him over by the swamp, past the gardens, animals, and fruit trees in one hour after they'd left. Gabriel figured the guys would head out, find a cozy spot to ditch the car and come back covertly on foot. After about forty-five minutes, Gabriel roused himself from the kitchen table, went to the bathroom, grabbed his coat and called for his dog.

"Humphrey, let's go for a walk before I go to bed. I know you haven't been out all night. Let's go."

The dog bounded over. The word "walk" was magical for pretty much every happy canine on the planet. And Humphrey was no exception. Gabriel grabbed a flashlight on his way out, along with a sharp knife just in case. In case what? He didn't know. Just, in case.

He wandered seemingly aimlessly, in the event he was being watched. Ultimately he made his way out towards the edge of the swamp. Moments after getting there, Humphrey growled a little. Then Gabriel saw Liam step out of the shadows and he calmed his dog. Then he walked over to where Liam stood.

"Joe is back aways. He's keeping a lookout. He'll buzz my cell, which is on vibrate, if he sees anything suspicious at all. Please talk to me Gabriel. We should be fine to do so now."

Gabriel started and he told Liam everything he knew about Lillian, her son, her past, their life together. Absolutely everything. The smallest and even the most private details. Liam stopped him often to clarify some of those details or ask more questions about certain points. It was grueling and exhausting. Never mind that it was really terribly painful for Gabriel.

Joe surfaced periodically, which cause Humphrey to growl periodically. That man didn't say much at all. He was an enigma. Silent, strong and wrung out weary all at the same time. Gabriel didn't pay him too much attention. His focus was on Liam. He had an innate sense that Liam could and would help him. Help Lillian. Help the boy. The dialogue, questions, and answers continued all through the night, well past the orange-pink glow of morning that infused through the kitchen windows. The men were all very tired at this point.

Humphrey stayed by Gabriel's side the entire time except for the moments when he had to go do his doggy business away from them every few hours. The dog knew there was something wrong.

After all the hours they spent together, by the time they were finished, Gabriel had painted a picture of a loving life he had made with his beautiful Lillian and her boy. He spoke of their dreams and wishes. Weary from their nocturnal activities the three men prepared to break company. At this point each man was silent and lost in his own thoughts. The men were startled out of their contemplations suddenly when Gabriel's cell phone rang. They all looked at each other. It was far too early for work or any other business to be calling a person. They waited silently, barely breathing, as Gabriel answered the call between the third and fourth ring.

"Hello."

The sick chuckle that Gabriel would learn to despise echoed through the phone line once again. "Well, well, well. How are we doing now sonny boy? Did you have a good night? Did you sleep well all alone in your beddy-by?" More sick chuckles followed. This motherfucker was getting off on this call, no doubt about it.

Gabriel was beyond patience and understanding at this point. He wanted his little family under his roof, safe and sound. He broke inside but wouldn't let it show. He straightened his spine, stood even more upright, and screamed into his phone. "Who are you, you mother fucking bastard? What do you want? Where's my Lillian? Where's my boy? What have you done to them? Where are they? What do you want? Tell me now!"

Both Liam and Joe tried to signal for him to calm down and keep the line open, keep the conversation going. Gabriel understood what they wanted him to do but struggled greatly to regain his composure in some elemental way.

The man at the other end of the phone gave yet another sinister laugh as he spoke, "I have a new surprise to share with you. Even I wasn't expecting one as juicy as this. And it is way too good to just keep to myself. My dear Gabriel, are you an angel as your name suggests? If so, I think you'd best reach out to your other angel friends to see if they can help you and save your family. You're going to need all the help you can get. Big time. Really big time. Are you ready yet sonny boy?" More sick chuckling ensued from his end.

Gabriel was sweating profusely at this point while also being chilled to his core. He swallowed hard and brought out whatever little bit of bluster he could choke out. "Bring it on you loser. Tell me what you've got for me."

The man on the phone laughed long and hard, chilling Gabriel even further.

"I don't think you're ready for this sonny boy. This one takes the cake. Let's see how you do with it. I'm on the edge of my seat for this one. Front row! I'm going to have this surprise delivered to you in style. Your lovely Lillian is going to explain everything to you. BUT. She has a very short window to do it in. AND. You are not allowed to ask her any questions. Your job is to just listen to the latest and greatest news. Oh this is just too good. I'm going to replay this one in my head for the rest of my life. This went beyond my wildest expectations. Tell me, have you guessed what it is yet?"

Gabriel pushed out a terse "No" and wished that somehow he could crawl through the phone line to get to this demonic man, whoever he was.

"Okay then. Like I said, no questions get to be asked of the lovely Lillian. Otherwise, I'm just going to hang up the phone and leave you, sonny boy, hanging. So, if you're really ready, HERE'S LILLIAN!"

Gabriel melted and died in so many different ways as he heard her soft sweet voice coming over the wire. She was such a part of him. His love. His soul mate. His lover. His best friend. And most of all, everything rolled in together because she was his wife. He fought back his tears and hung on to her every word.

"Gabriel? Are you there?" she asked. She sounded ever so weary. "My love, are you there?"

"Yes, I'm here sweetheart. I'm here. But I'm not allowed to ask you anything. But I'm here." Gabriel was so careful to choose words that wouldn't make the other guy hang up. He knew for a fact that if, no... when, he got her back, he was never ever going to let her go anywhere without him.

Gabriel had the phone on speaker by this point so Liam and Joe could hear the conversation. Then he heard the other guy in the background shouting, "Get on with it you bitch! Tell him your wonderful news flash or I will. But fucking hurry up!"

The men heard the sounds of body contact as Lillian's captor hit her a few more times. Her sobbing grew louder even though she tried to keep it in check. She choked back another sob before she spoke again. "I love you so much Gabriel. You have to know that. I hoped to come home tonight to tell you the wonderful news but then my world blew apart. You need to know that one of our dreams has come true. We're pregnant. We're going to have a baby. You're going to be a father to our own child. Gabriel, I'm so sorry you have to find out like this, but I need you. Please find us. Please help us. Please save us. Please. Please. Please, my love."

Gabriel could hear the phone being yanked from her hand. His head swam as he tried to digest what he'd just heard. He felt ill as he heard that sickening voice yet again. "Congratulations Daddy! Isn't that newsworthy? The fucking icing on the fucking cake! I hope you have a splendid day you fucking loser asshole! Bye Bye Daddy!"

Then came the final click as the call ended.

Gabriel just stared at his phone. Lost. Destroyed. Annihilated. Broken. Finished. The hum of a line with no connection continued.

The other men could do nothing but watch as Gabriel collapsed to his knees with his head in his hands.

Liam and Joe knew they could offer no words at this point to make Gabriel's pain go away, so they just looked on in a sympathetic and compassionate silence. The expressions on their faces showed their true feelings.

Humphrey whined and rested his doggy head on Gabriel's shoulder.

After quite some time, it was Liam who was the first to speak. "Gabriel, we need for all of us to get some rest, at least for a few hours, and then we need to figure out how to get your Lillian home. A fresh mind and fresher eyes will help us all. Please listen to me."

Gabriel raised his head at Liam's pleas and answered, "Who is going to make sure Lillian rests? Who is going to make sure she has food and water? Who is going to look after her? I can't rest until I know she's home safe. If you guys can't work any longer then bring on another shift. I have to find my pregnant wife and her son. I have to bring them home. I won't rest until she can."

Then Gabriel turned on his heels and walked back to his house with his dog at his side. A house that would not be a home until his wife and family were back. He was going to be a father. Oh, God, a father. His own flesh and blood. Lord, please look after Lillian, Stewart and my unborn baby. Gabriel pleaded with his Lord.

THIRTY THREE

CURRENT NIGHT

It took Liam a while to revive Gabriel. His skin was very white, his body shaking, and he was drenched in a cold sweat all over. Liam lifted him under his armpits from behind and half-lifted, half-dragged him over to the bed and onto it. Gabriel just fell back like a sick rag doll. Bogart jumped up and lay down on the pillow by Gabriel's head. He nudged and sniffed him, likely because of the odors coming off of his owner.

Liam walked quickly to the dresser and came back with a bottle of water for Gabriel. "Stay with me man. Here, sit up a bit and drink this." He forced him partially upright and then supported Gabriel's shoulders and back while the man downed some of the water. Gabriel lay back down again and Liam sat down next to him.

"We're going to figure this out my friend. Just please keep your head about you. And for God's sake, please stay with me here!" Liam's tone was simultaneously compassionate while having a hard edge to it.

Over the next few minutes, Gabriel's wits gradually returned to him, his breathing became more regulated and his skin color, although still very pale, was progressing from a whitish green to a sickly grey. He focussed on Liam's face and registered the concern on it. After another few minutes, Gabriel struggled to sit up, leaning heavily against the headboard, his pallor making its way towards something resembling normal. He desperately wanted to lie back down again, curl up into a fetal position, and simply just die. He didn't feel like he could handle this anymore. Instead, he issued a silent prayer and plea to God for strength and courage, for himself, his team, and his family. When he levelled his gaze on Liam he said, "I'm ready again. How do we fight now?"

At that moment Frank and Joe walked back into the room with some food bags and a few six packs. They hesitated, stopped talking, and stood silently just inside the room, innately sensing something was going on. Liam signalled them in and gestured for them to set up at the crappy excuse for a table in the room. They went about unpacking the food and drinks, then sat down, still not speaking.

"Get started, you two. We'll be right over." Then Liam turned his attention back to Gabriel. "I know you don't feel like it, but you need to eat a little, and a beer would do you some good too, to take the edge off. I need you nourished and your brain cannot work without food. Come on, let's go." He dragged Gabriel upright and over to a seat at the table, forced him to sit, handed him a beer and pushed some food in front of him.

Joe and Frank were devouring their food aggressively. They were obviously very hungry. Liam started on his dinner and ate much more slowly, with thoughts spinning through his head. He was wondering whether to tell Gabriel now or later what he'd learned earlier before all the shit hit the fan with that baby rattle thing. Fuck. Fuck. Fuck. What was the right thing to do?

Gabriel barely choked down a few bites of his food and took a few deliberate sips of the crappy warm local beer. The noise from the ineffective air conditioner and the men eating were the only sounds in the room. Bogart had jumped onto Gabriel's lap and was snacking on any meat pieces that were handed over to him. Survivor cat, with a few of his nine lives already gone. No one talked at all for several minutes after they were done eating and that silence was both deafening and grating. Then Liam briefed Frank and Joe about what had transpired while they were out. The boy with the bag and the phone call. The two men just listened quietly and absorbed the facts, both of them glancing at Gabriel occasionally, sympathetically.

After the short briefing, Gabriel looked at Liam and asked, "Tell me please Liam, what did the note say?" The look on Gabriel's face was palpable. He was begging for the information. Frank and Joe sat alert, waiting for the updates regarding what they'd walked in on.

Liam pushed his food away and took a slow long swig of the warm beer. He ran his hands across his head and sighed, "I don't want you to give up Gabriel. We're in this until we have all of the answers. What I'm going to tell you, I don't want to tell you, but I promised you from the very first day I met you that I'd tell you whatever I found out, so that's what I'm going to do. However, I want your word that you're going to stay strong so we can deal with this. Promise me that Gabriel, please."

"Yes, Liam, I promise to keep it together as best as I can. I'm fighting for my family." Then Gabriel swallowed hard, audibly and waited.

Liam pulled the note that had been in the bag with the blue baby rattle from his pocket and read it out loud. "Your baby boy doesn't need this anymore, Daddy. Consider it a keepsake from your son."

With that, Gabriel's world went entirely black again and he slid off the chair onto the floor, dislodging Bogart, and not for the first time either. The last words that registered in his brain before he passed out were "boy" and "daddy" and "son".

EPILOGUE

Have you wondered what has happened to Lillian during this entire time?

You've seen the world through Gabriel's eyes. What about her? And what about her little boy?

Strap on your seat belts if you have the stomach to hear their story in *The Mother & The Monster.*

It will be on bookshelves soon.

CPSIA information can be obtained
at www.ICGtesting.com
Printed in the USA
LVOW10*2015280917
550425LV00005BA/157/P